THE DRIVING LESSON

For Tristan & Hayden.

THE DRIVING LESSON

Ben Rehder

Acknowledgments

I'd like to thank the following people for making this a better book: Mary Summerall, Stacia Hernstrom, Becky Rehder, Helen Haught Fanick, Marsha Moyer, Tommy Blackwell, John Grace, Roxanne Tea, and Allan Kimball. And thanks to Laurence Parent for the cover photo.

THE DRIVING LESSON

1

If, during the last week of my freshman year, you'd asked me what I was planning to do that summer, I can guarantee you that becoming a fugitive would not have made the list. Not even a really long list. Especially if you'd told me that I wouldn't be alone, that it would be me and my grandfather — seriously, my *Opa* — together, on the run, the subject of a nationwide manhunt. *Yeah, right,* I would've said. *Are you friggin' nuts?*

But, as we know now, that's exactly what happened. Events sort of conspired, as Mr. Gardner, my English teacher, would say. And before the entire fiasco was over, we'd become an international phenomenon. The chaos would grow to include...

Cops across Texas asking the public for help in tracking us down.

Newspapers from Los Angeles to New York plastering our photos all over the front page, me with my baby face and blondish-white hair.

John Walsh talking about us on *America's Most Wanted*,

stressing that we were most likely unarmed. Most likely?

People tweeting about us, talking about us on Facebook, posting videos on YouTube that supposedly showed us eating breakfast at an Iowa truck stop or camping out at Big Bend National Park.

My parents, Glen and Sarah Dunbar, appearing on CNN, Mom pleading for God to deliver "her baby Charlie" home safely, while Dad sits there looking uncomfortable and the smoking hot newsbabe nods with sympathy.

So, yeah, you can kind of understand why I didn't see any of this coming. Silly me, I thought the highlight of my summer would be getting my learner's permit.

The last Saturday in May plays an important role in this story, because that's when Matt, my best friend, talked me into doing something really dumb. Actually, two dumb things in a row, the second one worse than the first.

It was about thirty minutes before dark and we were walking to the bowling alley. Yeah, it sounds lame. Who bowls, right? But it's something Matt has done since he was about five, and I've known Matt since third grade, so I usually tag along, and sometimes I bowl, too. My high score is 114. Matt's is 223. So you can tell which one of us applies himself.

Anyway, we were walking past a home under construction on the edge of the neighborhood where we both live. There aren't many empty lots left in our subdivision, but every so often, one of the remaining lots sells and a new home gets slapped up in a matter of a few months. We're not talking high-dollar mansions, just tract homes that look like all the rest in the area. This particular home was nearly complete, and there was already a for-sale sign stuck in the freshly sodded yard. *I'm gorgeous inside!* the sign proclaimed. (My dad joked that that sounded like the title for a book designed to build self-esteem in teenage girls.)

That's when Matt stopped walking and said, "Charlie, check it out." He was looking at the house.

"What?"

"The front door is open."

And it was. Wide open. Like somebody forgot to lock it and the wind had given it a shove. The construction workers were gone for the day. The place was quiet and still.

I stopped, too. So what if the door was open? Nothing good could come from going inside a home under construction, especially since we'd gotten into trouble less than a month ago for skipping an assembly at school. Under those circumstances, only an idiot would go inside this house.

Matt said, "Let's go inside."

"Forget it."

"Just for a minute."

"Why?"

"Why not?"

"It's stupid."

"I just want to look around."

"Be my guest."

"Come with me."

"Nope."

"It'll be fun."

"It'll be trespassing."

"Don't be a pussy."

And there it was. Matt's trump card. Whenever he wanted to push my buttons, he'd call me a pussy. I *hated* it and he knew it. But, of course, my only option was to act like I didn't care, or he'd still be calling me that name when we were living in a retirement home. So I said, "Whatever, dude."

"Pussy."

"Real mature."

"Pussy."

"Jeez, Matt, grow the hell up."

"Pussy."

"You might want to broaden your vocabulary."

"Pussy."

I knew from experience that it wouldn't do any good to keep arguing with him. He can be a persistent little jerk. So, even though I wish I could go back and do that night over — use some common sense — instead, well, you can probably see where this is going.

We closed the front door behind us and stood there for a few seconds in the tiled entry hallway, which would be called a foyer in a larger home. I have to admit, my heart was pumping pretty good. We weren't supposed to be in here, but we were, and it was exciting. Exhilarating, even.

"Come on," Matt said, and he stepped slowly into the living room, onto the carpet, which was clean and perfect. The entire house was spotless. I could smell fresh paint.

But something was strange. Sort of familiar. Then I figured it out. I whispered, "You know what? This place has the exact same floor plan as my house."

And it did. Dining room over there. Three bedrooms down that hallway. Fireplace with a window on either side. Weird. It made me wonder how many other homes in the neighborhood were just like mine — except maybe with a different coat of paint on the outside, or bricks instead of plywood siding.

Matt didn't say anything. He was just looking around with this odd little grin on his face. Enjoying the rush. The light was fading as the sun was beginning to set, but I noticed that his sneakers were leaving smudges on the carpet.

"Let's go, Matt," I said.

"Not yet."

"There's nothing to see in here. The place is empty."

No response.

"Matt!"

He moved toward a swinging door on the other side of the living room. I knew that was the way to the kitchen, just like in my house. Matt went through the door, but I stayed behind, near one of the windows, so I could keep an eye on the street.

I was starting to get nervous. What if someone had seen us come in? It wasn't like we were real sly about it, walking right up to the front door. Anyone watching would've known we didn't belong in here. Which could mean the police might be on their way right this very minute.

"Matt!"

If we got caught...I didn't even want to think how my mom would respond.

Suddenly Matt, still in the kitchen, said, "Sweet!" And here he came through the door again, holding something. "Dude, look what I found."

It was a cordless drill. My dad had one like it, but a different brand. Yellow instead of blue. I was with him at Home Depot when he bought it. Nearly two hundred bucks, which is a lot of money.

"Put it back," I said.

"Somebody must've forgot it."

"Quit screwing around."

He pulled the trigger on the drill and it made a powerful whirring sound. It seemed awfully loud in the quiet house.

"Man, I could *use* this!" Matt said.

"For what?"

"Stuff."

"Don't even think about it."

But he had that grin on his face again. Sometimes I hate that grin.

At this point, I should mention that I outweigh Matt by about thirty pounds. I'm nearly six feet tall, one of the biggest kids in the freshman class, and sometimes my size has its advantages. Like making nose guard on the football team. Or like right now. If I had to, I could wrestle the drill away from Matt and put it back in the kitchen. Then we'd leave. Sure, Matt would be pissed, but he'd get over it. Later, he'd realize how dumb it would've been to steal the drill. He'd realize that I'd actually done him a favor. So that was the plan, to try to talk him out of it, and if that didn't work, to use my superior physical attributes to impose my will.

And that's when we heard the car door out front.

Here's what would happen if I got caught.

I'd get grounded, for sure — probably for at least a month, and maybe for the entire summer. No cell phone, no computer, no video games, no TV, no iPod. No hanging out at the mall, no riding my bike, no going to the movies, no having friends over to share in my misery. Guess what I'd be expected to do instead?

Read the Bible.

Seriously. My mom would insist on it. Didn't matter that I'd already read it several times, cover to cover, in my nearly fifteen years. When I was younger, parts of it sort of freaked me out, especially in the Old Testament. I mean, come on — people think *Mortal Kombat* is gruesome? The Bible has this big long list of reasons to stone people to death. It's got plagues, brought on by God, that wipe out entire cities, plus human and animal sacrifices, fathers having sex with their daughters, and a bunch of other bizarre events. Kind of disturbing when you're a kid. Now that I'm older, frankly, it just bores me. But Sarah Dunbar — that's my mother — is a firm believer that reading the Bible can cure all ills. The King James version, of course.

Any time I got in trouble, even for something relatively

minor, like being tardy to class, she'd say something like, "I didn't raise you to be a juvenile delinquent," and then she'd pronounce my punishment. Could be a few verses, a couple of chapters, or even a full book. If she was really angry, I'd have to write a report about what I'd learned, assuming I'd had any luck deciphering what I'd read.

So maybe you can understand just how badly I didn't want to get caught in that house.

Matt's eyes got really big. I'm sure mine did, too.

I peeked out the window and saw a green Ford Explorer parked at the curb. A woman was coming around the front of the SUV, walking slowly, because she was in the middle of a conversation on her cell phone. She was about my parents' age, dressed nicely in a skirt and high heels. Everything about her said real estate agent. She was in charge of selling this house. She probably had some clients coming to look at the place right now.

"Oh, crap," I said, because I'm such a master of the English language. Now my heart was really pounding.

"Who is it?" Matt hissed. He hadn't moved.

"Some lady. Maybe a realtor."

"Is she coming in?"

"She...she..."

"She what?"

"She's stopping at the for-sale sign. It has one of those little boxes for flyers. She's checking to see if there are any flyers left."

Matt came up behind me and peeked over my shoulder. I was beginning to feel sick. "This is your fault," I said.

"Maybe that's all she came for, to check the flyers. Maybe she'll drive away."

The real-estate lady, still talking on her phone, let the

metal lid slap shut on the rectangular box. Then she started up the driveway toward the house.

I turned quickly. "Follow me," I said.

He did, too. Amazing how, all of a sudden, Matt was willing to listen to a pussy like me. He was too frozen with fear to realize that all we had to do was go out the back door, which we did, closing that door just as we heard the front door opening.

It wasn't until we'd ducked through a gate in the privacy fence and started jogging down the street that I noticed Matt was still carrying the cordless drill.

I got home around nine-thirty, and I halfway expected my parents to be waiting for me, looking stern, ready to tear me a new one, because I just knew the cops had already solved the crime and had come to the house looking for me.

I'm a wimp that way, a total bundle of nerves when it comes to the possibility of getting in trouble — so much so that my mom can usually tell just from looking at my face that I've been up to something.

But that didn't turn out to be a problem tonight, because my parents were nowhere to be seen when I came through the front door. Normally, one or both of them would be hanging out in the living room, watching TV or reading. Or Mom would be busy in the kitchen while Dad was in the study working or just goofing around on the computer.

Then I heard them, just a low murmuring from their bedroom. The lights were on in the hallway. I decided I'd just duck into their doorway, say a quick goodnight, and go to bed before my own behavior gave me away. Then I began to wonder if going to bed so quickly would be a giveaway in itself. Maybe it would be better to talk to them for longer than a few seconds. Sheesh.

I started down the hallway. *Just act normal. Be yourself. Don't be an idiot.*

I was literally two steps from their bedroom door — and they still didn't know I'd come home — when I heard my mother say, "Here? Honey, you know that won't work. He'll have to end up in hospice."

Now she saw me in the doorway, and I saw them sitting on the edge of the bed, holding hands.

"Charlie," she said. That, and nothing else. It was strange, the way she said my name, and the odd expression on her face. Like she was surprised to see me. No, that's not exactly right. She looked like I'd caught her doing something she shouldn't be doing, or maybe saying something she didn't want me to hear.

"I'm home," I announced. Well, duh.

My dad looked up and caught my eye, but only for a second. He was acting weird, too. Angry about something? Sad? Were his eyes red?

"How was bowling?" Mom asked.

"Okay." Not really. I'd scored an 82, with three gutter balls. My mind had been on other things, like the fact that I'd taken part in a burglary.

Dad got up and went into the bathroom. Mom looked at me and gave a weak smile. "How is Matt?"

"Fine." *Despite being a felon in training.*

"Are you hungry? There's some pizza left in the fridge."

She's always trying to feed me — I'm a big guy and I burn a lot of calories — but I got the distinct impression she was making small talk to sort of gloss over the odd vibe in the air.

Had my parents been arguing about something? Or about somebody? And what in the heck was a hospice? I knew it had something to do with nurses or hospitals. Which meant there could only be one person they were talking about.

2

My phone chimed at 8:37 the next morning. A text message from Matt.

Any prblms?

I'd been awake for nearly an hour, but I was still in bed, just thinking about things. About last night. Not so much about the stolen drill, but about "hospice care." I'd looked it up on the Internet and was not happy with what I'd learned.

Yeah, there are problems, I thought.

That was made even more obvious by the fact that church started at nine and it appeared we weren't going. Mom hadn't even knocked on my door to get me up for breakfast. I didn't smell bacon frying or coffee brewing. In fact, I didn't hear any movement or talking at all in the house.

I lay there for several minutes, just feeling crummy. To be honest, I was kind of enjoying leaving Matt hanging. He was always doing stupid stuff and somehow getting me involved. Like this thing with the drill. So I texted him back.

Cops came this morning

His reply came within fifteen seconds:

Srius?

I could picture the panic he was feeling. Pretty funny.

I denied evrythng

Not funny

Not a joke

I put my phone on silent mode because I knew what he'd do next, and sure enough, it rang. I let it go to voicemail. Thirty seconds passed. Then he sent a text:

Where r u

Cant talk now

Im freaking out whats happening

Cops r chcking the nborhood door 2 door

U r lying

Wish i was

OMG 4 a stupid drill?

Doesnt mttr its stil theft

The door was open

Rmembr whn ur bike was stolen?

Now there was a long pause and I realized I had a huge smile on my face. I was getting him good. Last year, somebody had taken Matt's mountain bike when he'd left it in front of a convenience store. His dad had been really pissed that he'd left it unlocked and wouldn't buy him a new one. That's why we walked everywhere now — Matt had no bike.

Finally he said: *Shld we put it back?*

That caught me by surprise. Put the drill back? I thought about it, then said: *Door wont be unlocked now*

Cld leave it on back porch

Might get caught

We'd b careful

Not we, u

U wont go?

No

Plz go w me

U stole it u return it

I need a lookout
Good luck
Y r u being such a jerk

Was I? Maybe I was. Regardless, I was tired of stringing him along. And he deserved to know what was really going on, since he was my best friend. So I said:

Think my g'father is dying

Later, I found Mom in the living room, folding sheets and watching Pat Robertson, and she acted as if everything was fine. When I asked why we hadn't gone to church, she said Dad hadn't been feeling well when he woke up, so she let him sleep late. Then she asked if I was hungry, and before I could even answer, she said, "Of course you are," and went into the kitchen to make me some breakfast.

She seemed awfully cheerful. Maybe I was wrong about Opa. That's what we called him, because of his mother's German ancestry. Maybe I'd misheard what Mom had said last night, or maybe they'd been talking about someone else.

I was even more convinced of that when, a couple hours later, Dad finally emerged from his bedroom — fully dressed, apparently feeling much better — and said, "Grab the keys, Charlie!"

"Huh?"

"Time for another driving lesson!"

"Parallel parking," Dad said very seriously, "is the most important part of the test."

He was bending down to look at me through the passenger window. It was a long way down for him, because he's six foot four. I get my size from his side of the family.

Dad continued, saying, "When I was your age, it counted

for a full thirty points. So if you screwed it up, the best you could get was a seventy, which meant you were just one point — one measly point — from a failing grade." His voice was rising with mock outrage. He was kidding around because he has a weird sense of humor. I think he got it from Opa, who is even more of a goofball. Dad went on. "It didn't matter if you drove with the precision of Richard Petty and the skill of Dale Earnhardt, if you couldn't parallel park like you'd been doing it all your life, you didn't get your license. Personally, I don't think that's very reasonable, but that's the way it was. What're you gonna do? Bunch of bureaucrats."

I couldn't help grinning at him. "That's what happened to you, huh, Dad?"

"Is it that obvious? Yeah, well, my instructor was a hard-ass."

He used words like that sometimes when Mom wasn't around. It was understood that this was a guy thing, only between us.

"Okay, you ready to give it a try?" he asked.

We were in the huge parking lot of the exposition center on the east side of town. This is where they held the rodeo, dog shows, tractor pulls, and various concerts, but no events were taking place today, so it was a ghost town.

The parking lot was basically a wide-open expanse of pavement, with the occasional curbed island of concrete here and there to divide the big lot into smaller sections. We'd come here for previous lessons, and Dad had taught me the basics — shifting gears smoothly, braking hard without locking up the tires, backing up for a long distance — all the things that would be on the driving test.

Today, Dad had placed a pair of orange traffic cones exactly twenty-five feet apart, with each cone about six feet out from a long, straight section of curb. It was my job to parallel park our Toyota between those two cones.

I didn't know why he was making such a big deal out of it. It looked simple enough. He had already demonstrated for me a couple of times. As you back up, he said, you whip the wheel this way, then, at just the right moment, you whip it the other way, and presto, you slide right into the slot. Take it slow. Keep an eye on the cones.

Piece of cake, I thought. *No problem. It's not trigonometry.*

On my first try, I totally crushed the cone in front.

Dad was ready with some sound effects. He screamed like I'd just run over a pedestrian. "Aaah! Oh, my God, help me! My leg! You crushed my leg!"

Yeah, okay, I'll admit I laughed. Then I pulled out, he stood the cone up again, and I gave it another shot. I whipped it too late and rolled over the rear cone. Another pedestrian. It was like I was playing *Grand Theft Auto.*

Dad said, "For the love of God, somebody stop this maniac! An ambulance! I need an ambulance!"

Right about then, I was grateful there wasn't another soul within a mile of us. It was embarrassing.

The third time, with some verbal coaching from Dad, I did a little better. Didn't hit a cone, but wound up parked about three feet from the curb. You're supposed to be eighteen inches or closer.

But I got better with each try. After about a dozen attempts, I finally nailed it.

"There you go! Now you've got it!"

Three more times in a row, I managed to park without sending any imaginary pedestrians to the hospital or the morgue. It felt good.

Dad climbed into the passenger seat and closed the door. "You know what? I'm thinking you should drive us home today."

"Really?" That would be cool. I hadn't driven on any real streets yet, just this parking lot.

"Yeah, we'll take the back streets. No highways. Think you can handle that?"

"I think so, yeah."

"I do, too. You're getting the hang of it. I'm proud of you. But first, why don't you cut the engine for minute. We need to talk about something."

I knew immediately what was coming.

The word "grandpa" might bring to mind a certain image for some people: a little white-haired guy with arthritis and poor hearing. My grandfather wasn't like that at all. Not even close.

Yeah, he was sixty-three years old — getting up there — but he was very active, always running around doing something. Like he was a big-time swimmer. Went to a public pool in his neighborhood four or five mornings a week. He played the guitar and wrote his own songs. He attended political rallies and book signings and all kinds of fundraisers.

He dated a lot, too. He and my grandmother had gotten a divorce before I was even born, and Opa had never remarried. Instead, he had what my mother called "lady friends."

He traveled with some of these friends to other states and even other countries. Just last summer, he went to Ireland with a redheaded woman named Linda. A couple years before that, he went to Africa with a woman whose name I can't remember. For a while after that trip, he wore a shirt called a *dashiki*. It had all these wild colors, and I thought it looked pretty cool, but my mom always said he looked like some old nut. Other times, when she was being nicer, she used the word "eccentric."

My point is, he wasn't some decrepit geezer ready for a nursing home. Heck, he had more energy than me and most of my friends. Or he used to.

***

"You know that Opa hasn't been feeling good."

I nodded.

Dad said, "He...well, for a while, nobody could say what was wrong with him. The doctors didn't know. He just didn't feel right, so they ran various tests, and everything looked okay. They said he was probably fine, just getting old, and he shouldn't worry too much about it. We told you about that. Remember right after Christmas?"

My face was starting to feel very warm. I nodded again. I did remember. First they told me Opa might be sick, then they said maybe he wasn't, then, just before spring break, they said it was a "wait and see" type of thing. We hadn't really talked much about it since then.

"In early April," Dad said, "he went to a special hospital in Houston. It's one of the best in the country. They ran even more tests, different tests, and this time they were able to figure out what the problem is." He paused for a second. "Unfortunately, it wasn't good news. He has a type of bone cancer that is very aggressive. It's already in the advanced stages."

Does it make me a pussy to admit my eyes were starting to fill with tears? A real tough guy, right? Big football player. Macho and all that. But cancer is scary. Everybody knows that.

I was looking down at my lap. My dad had his arm on the driver's headrest behind me. Now he placed his hand on my neck, rubbing it, trying to make me feel better, but I was this close to bawling like a baby. Some snot dripped from my nose and landed on my jeans.

Dad said, "It gets a little more complicated, because Opa has some wild ideas about what he should do next. He isn't thinking straight. Maybe it's his age, or maybe he's just scared, but he's decided that he doesn't want to undergo the treatment plan the doctors are recommending."

Now I looked up. "Why not?"

"Well, it can be pretty rough on the patient. And the chances that it would be successful are pretty slim. It comes down to what they call 'quality of life.'"

I knew the answer, but I asked the question anyway. "Is he going to die?"

I don't know whether my dad had decided hours ago to be completely honest with me, or if he made the decision right then and there. But when I think back on this moment, as painful as it was, I'm glad he didn't sugarcoat it or give me any false hope.

He simply said, "Yeah, he is."

Now the tears really began to flow.

He said, "I'm sorry, Charlie. I'm really sorry. Even with the treatment, he...that would only delay it, or maybe it wouldn't even do that."

Now he was getting emotional, too, and I couldn't bring myself to look at him. I looked down at my lap again, and we just sat there for another minute or two, neither of us saying anything.

Then, when I thought I could talk without blubbering, I said, "How soon?"

3

I know this sounds strange, but before my dad and I left that parking lot, we were laughing hysterically. That's because, after he answered that question and several others, and after we both cried quite a bit, we started talking about Opa — remembering some of the things he'd said or done over the years.

Like the time he was showing us all a yoga move he'd learned and he ripped an enormous fart. Opa wasn't embarrassed by it at all — he said it was perfectly natural — but Mom got grossed out and left the room.

Or the time Opa decided to return a shirt he'd gotten as a gift. The sales clerk at the department store started to say they couldn't take the shirt, so Opa interrupted and gave a big speech about how consumers are more important than big corporations, and how the clerk's failure to accept the shirt symbolized the problem with excessive greed in this country, and that's when the clerk interrupted and said, "I'm sorry, sir, but that shirt isn't from this store."

Funny things like that.

Dad said we'd always have those memories, and I know

I'm only fourteen — almost fifteen — but that didn't sound like much, really. I didn't want memories, I wanted Opa, in the flesh, right here for a long time to come.

Then, as I was driving home (which sort of reminded me of sneaking into the empty house yesterday, because it was exciting, but I was also a little worried about getting caught by a cop), Dad said, "Uh, maybe you should pull over a block or two before we get home and let me drive the rest of the way."

I nodded. He didn't want Mom to see that I was driving without a license. So that's what we did — switched seats when we were almost home.

It's a good thing, too. Because there's an excellent chance I would've freaked out and wrecked when I saw the SUV that was parked at the curb in front of our house. It was a green Ford Explorer. Just like the one I'd seen last night.

And there, on the front porch, was the real-estate lady, having a conversation with my mom.

Dad parked in the driveway.

Was I panicking? Oh, absolutely. Palms beginning to sweat. Heart pounding. About to crap my underwear. I wanted to hunker down in the passenger seat and not get out, but that would've been the same as admitting my guilt. For all I knew, the real-estate lady was asking my mom if we wanted to sell our home. Yeah, right. I didn't believe that for a second.

Dad got out of the car, so I did too, and I followed behind him on the sidewalk to the porch, hoping I was all but invisible.

My hands were trembling.

Mom and the lady were talking, and as we got closer, Mom said, "Here's my husband. Honey, this is Cathy..."

"Abbott," the lady said.

Dad shook her hand. "Glen Dunbar."

"Nice to meet you," Cathy Abbott said. She pointed

vaguely with her right hand. "I live on the other side of the neighborhood."

Dad said, "Yeah, you're the realtor, right? I've seen your name on the signs."

"That's me," she said, smiling. She was wearing the same sort of outfit as last night: a skirt and a colorful blouse. Up close, I could tell she was probably a little younger than my parents. She was actually very pretty, in an overdone kind of way. Lots of makeup and jewelry.

Dad turned a little sideways, toward me, and said, "This is our son, Charlie."

She looked at me. I looked at her. Her smile remained in place, but something changed. She was *studying* me, I think.

"Hi," I said.

"Nice to meet you, Charlie."

I looked away, but I could feel Cathy Abbott's eyes lingering on me. I noticed that Mom was looking at Dad with an expression on her face that basically said, *Did everything go okay?* She was wondering how our conversation about Opa went.

There was an awkward silence, until Cathy Abbott said to my dad, "I was telling Sarah about a little, oh, incident we had yesterday. A minor crime wave, you might call it. You know that home under construction on the corner of LaSalle and Miller's Loop?"

Dad nodded. "That red brick house."

"Right. Well, I have that listing, and I stopped there last night at about eight. Just before dark. The front door was unlocked, and just as I stepped inside, I heard the back door close. At first I thought one of the construction workers was still there, but then I saw two people — teenage boys, I think — through one of the windows in the kitchen. They went through a gate and took off. There wasn't any damage to the house, but this morning I found out that a couple of things were stolen."

A couple of things? What was she talking about? It was only one thing.

She looked at me again. Actually, I think she was checking out my hair. See, I have extremely blond hair, almost white, and it's very curly and thick. A big mop. Fairly unmistakable. If she saw me through a window, even for just a second, the thing she'd most likely remember is my hair. I was really wishing I'd worn a hat today. Instead, I did my best to look like any other innocent teenager, but I don't think I did a very good job. My face felt like it was turning bright red.

Dad said, "Did you call the police?"

Cathy Abbott said, "No, not yet. I'm just going door to door, hoping maybe I can figure it out without getting the authorities involved. I don't want to get some kids in major trouble. I'm pretty sure burglary is a felony. Or breaking and entering. I'm not sure what the charge would be."

Dad said, "Why don't you give us your card, and if we hear anything — "

But Mom interrupted and said, "What did these boys look like?"

Time sort of froze for a second. I wanted to run away. Seriously, just take off down the street and never come back. Cathy Abbott didn't seem to know who to answer first. She opened her mouth, started to say something, then changed her mind and said, "They were both in shorts and T-shirts. One of the boys was pretty tall, maybe six feet. He had very blond hair. Curly hair."

Crap, crap, crap!

Cathy Abbott looked at me again.

Mom turned and looked at me.

Dad, however, did not. I'm sure he thought about it. I mean, if it was possible, *I* would've turned and looked at me. It was that obvious, that Cathy Abbott was implying that it might've been me in the empty house last night. But, no, Dad didn't budge. He said, "Cathy, the truth is, we're in the middle of a family crisis at the moment — my father is very sick — so if you'll leave us your card — "

And once again, my mother interrupted.

"Charlie, do you know anything about this?"

Remember when I said I'm a wimp when it comes to the possibility of getting in trouble? Part of the reason for that is my mom's tone. When she wants to know something, her voice becomes like this needle of anger and disappointment that she inserts deep into my skin, jabbing me, prodding me, making it clear that the situation will not go away until the truth is known. She *demands* the truth. Especially when she thinks she already knows the answer, as she plainly did here.

I opened my mouth, but nothing came out.

Dad said, "Seriously, this isn't a good time for this."

Mom said, "Charlie, were you in that house? You and Matt?"

I have to hand it to Cathy Abbott. By this point, she actually appeared to feel sorry for me. She even made a small move toward the porch steps, as if to leave, and she said, "Maybe I should just — "

"Charlie?" Mom said. Her voice was getting louder. She wanted an answer, right this minute. "Were you in that house or not?"

This was it. The moment of truth.

You know how I finally responded? This totally blew me away. I said, "No, ma'am. Absolutely not. You and Dad raised me better than that."

You have to understand — in our house, there are very few offenses held in more contempt than lying. Now, of course, I'm not including things like murder and armed robbery. But as far as teenager type of behavior, bearing false witness was perhaps the greatest sin. If you skip a class, that's bad. If you lie about it, that's even worse. Lying brings more shame on your head than smoking a cigarette or cussing or even whacking off.

But in the last year or so, I'd come up with a theory: Maybe Mom condemned lying with such vehemence simply so that I'd *admit* to those other things.

For some reason, standing there on the porch, facing an inquisition, I'd decided that wasn't going to happen this time. Maybe I was protecting Matt. Maybe I was being selfish and only protecting myself. Or maybe, just once, I didn't think Mom needed to know all my secrets. After all, I was nearly fifteen years old. I could fix this mess myself. Matt and I would return the drill and be done with it. I'd learned my lesson, and wasn't that the important thing?

Mom stared at me hard, and I can tell you this much: She wasn't buying it at all. Not even the tiniest bit.

"Charlie," she said slowly, "Cathy is being very reasonable about this situation. If you know anything about it — anything at all — now's the time to tell us, before it goes any farther."

In other words, *last chance, buddy boy.* I'd already peeked over the cliff. Might as well jump.

I said, "I didn't do it and I don't know who did. End of story." Then, just for grins, I added, "You know something? I'm not the only kid in the world with blond hair."

Then I walked inside. Just like that, before anyone could ask me any more questions. As I slipped past my dad, I noticed the slightest trace of a grin on his face.

Pretty cool, huh? I thought so. But right before I closed the door behind me, I heard my mom say, "Well, Cathy, I guess you have no choice but to call the police."

I went to my bedroom and immediately texted Matt.
Call me

Cant. In car w m&d wats up?

So I sent him a series of messages that explained the situation.

I told him about Cathy Abbott, and how she had seen us through a window, and that it was pretty obvious, when she met me, that she thought I was one of the kids in the house.

I told him about my mother's questions, and how I had lied, and how my mom had told Cathy Abbott to go ahead and call the cops.

I said that as long as we kept our story straight and denied going into the house, nobody could prove anything, but he should also return the drill as soon as possible, if he could figure out how to do it without getting caught.

And last, I said this absolutely was not a joke, and then I called him a pinhead for getting us into this mess, because it was a moronic thing to do, and if we did get busted, I'd expect him to tell the cops that it was all his idea.

When I was finally done, he sent me a one-word reply: *Sorry.*

I said: *Thats OK, delete these msgs*

My plan was to hole up in my room all day, pretending to be hurt by my mother's accusations. Besides, I had studying to do, because I had one more final exam tomorrow, Monday. Despite the fact that I appeared to be a punk on the road to hell, or at least prison, I was actually a pretty good student and I wanted to keep my grades up.

The question was, would my mother leave me alone or would she come up and keep grilling me? I figured it could go either way.

At one point, about thirty minutes after the incident on the porch, I could hear raised voices. My parents were having an intense conversation, also known as an argument. They didn't have many of those. It only lasted about five minutes. After that, they might've still been fighting, but if they were, they were doing it quietly.

It was an hour later when my mother finally did show up. She knocked softly on the door, then opened it. I was sitting at my desk, trying to read a web site about the Byzantine Empire without my eyes glazing over. So far, it wasn't working.

Mom leaned against the doorjamb, going for a casual look. Odd, isn't it, that you get to know your parents' body language so well that you can tell what kind of conversation you're about to have?

She said, "How you doing?"

"Fine."

She looked past me, to my computer screen. "What're you studying?"

"The fall of Constantinople."

"Oh, boy, I remember that. Thrilling stuff, huh?" Trying to lighten the mood with sarcasm. Parents were never very good at it. Well, my dad was, but most parents weren't.

"World History final," I said.

Tomorrow was the last day of school. Normally, it would have been two days ago, on Friday, but they'd had to add one extra day because of a snow day earlier in the year.

"And then you're all done, huh?"

"Yep."

Mom nodded, and now the small talk was out of the way, so she could move on to other things, which she did. "Listen, I just wanted to see how you're doing after your talk with Dad this morning. How are you handling it?"

"I'm okay."

She did that thing she does, lowering her head, moving it, trying to catch my eye. "You sure?"

I nodded again.

"Do you have any questions about his condition or...?"

"No, Dad pretty much covered it."

"Okay, good. It's a very sad situation, but we wanted to be completely up front with you about it. There are no easy answers, so remember to include Opa in your prayers tonight."

Somehow she managed to fool herself into thinking I still prayed every night, or at all, anywhere, unless I was in church, although all I really do there is lower my head. But I wasn't about to tell her that.

She said, "We think it would be a good idea if we all went to see Opa tomorrow evening. He needs us right now. I'll make a casserole and we'll take it over there. So come home right after school, okay? He likes to eat early."

"Okay."

Then — maybe I should've known this was coming — she said, "About this thing with the house down the street...I'm sorry if I hurt your feelings on the porch earlier, but if you took those things, the best thing to do is admit it, because God already knows the truth."

I was thinking, *Seriously? Right after we talk about Opa, we're going to keep talking about this?* I didn't miss a beat. I said, "That's cool, because it means He knows I didn't do it. Too bad *you* don't believe me."

It sounded snottier than I meant it to. But, to be technical, I was telling the truth. *I* didn't take "those things," Matt did. Plus, it was only one thing, and he was going to put it back.

Mom frowned. "As I said, if you didn't do it, then I apologize."

I just shook my head and turned back toward my computer. She didn't say anything, so I said, "I've got studying to do." Just as snotty.

After a few seconds, I heard the door close.

When I think back on it, I wish I hadn't been such a jerk. I should've just kept quiet. Because now Mom thought I was mad at her, and later she would probably even start to wonder if she was being unfair. Which meant she would feel responsible when I vanished without a trace after school the next day.

4

I walked out the front door of the school and saw Opa.

And this is when it all began — all the craziness that I've been talking about. Right here, right now. Of course, I didn't know that at the time. All I saw was my grandfather leaning against his Honda Civic. He was dressed in some khakis and a long-sleeved shirt, even though it was nearly eighty degrees. Even from this distance, maybe forty yards, I could tell that he was skinnier than the last time I'd seen him.

I stood there on the steps for a second, a little confused, wondering why he was here. He hadn't seen me yet, because the front of the building was swarming with kids, all of them excited about school letting out for the summer.

Then he saw me and raised his hand. He smiled.

I walked over with my backpack slung over my shoulder. Yeah, he was definitely skinnier, and kind of pale. And I noticed he was holding a cane. I didn't know what to say, so it's a good thing he spoke first.

"Learn anything good today, Bud?"

That was what he always called me. Bud, or sometimes Buddy. As far as I knew, there was no particular reason for it.

"Not really," I said.

"Crap, you're kidding me. My tax dollars are going down the toilet. You didn't learn anything at all?"

"Just the regular stuff."

"Here's something: Did you know that there are only forty-six states in the United States?"

He's always coming up with weird little facts about history and science and stuff. "Okay, what's the trick?" I asked.

"No trick. It's just that four of the 'states' are actually commonwealths."

I shook my head. "Oh, man."

"What, you didn't like that one?"

"You've had better. Besides, I don't even know what a commonwealth is."

"Well, you can look it up on that fancy Internet thing you kids use."

He was a goofball and a teaser. I think he surfed the Internet more than I did.

"So, what, uh, what're you doing here?"

He said, "I tried to call you earlier but I got voicemail."

"We have to turn our phones off during school or they'll take them away for a week."

"Oh, yeah? Probably a pretty good rule."

Something wasn't quite right. I knew that.

"Is there like an emergency or something?"

"No, no. Nothing like that. Everything's fine. I just need a favor."

"Yeah? What's up?"

"First things first, we might as well acknowledge the elephant in the room. I understand your dad had a talk with you yesterday, so you know my situation. No need to dwell on that. But the thing is, I need you to drive me to a doctor's appointment."

"What? When?"

"Right now."

"But...I don't have my learner's permit yet."

"You can drive, can't you? Your dad's been giving you lessons. I hear you're hell on wheels."

It felt good to know that Dad had been bragging about me. "I'm pretty good."

"You won't hit a tree or anything, right? Trees rarely move, so it's pretty easy to avoid them."

"Funny, but it's the other cars on the road I'm worried about."

"I have enough confidence in you for the both of us."

I have to admit it all seemed a little odd. Opa could obviously still drive. He drove here, didn't he? I gestured toward the side of the school. "But I have my bike."

He thought about that for a second. "We'll bring it."

"But you don't have a bike rack."

"We'll put it in the back. Lay the seat down, it'll be fine. Plenty of room. I bet we could fit a family of circus clowns back there."

So that's what we did. I went to get my bike, and when I came back, Opa was sitting in the passenger's seat. He had already popped the hatch, and there, shoved to one side of the cargo space, was a suitcase.

Big clue.

Enormous clue.

There might as well have been a flashing red arrow pointing at it.

Just as I started to ask what the suitcase was for, Opa said, "Load 'er up, Bud. Let's get rolling."

We took Mockingbird down to South First and turned right, going west. We passed Leggett, then Pioneer — both major intersections — but we kept going straight. Then we passed under Winters Freeway. It wasn't much farther to the edge of town.

"Uh, where is this doctor's office, Opa?"

"Just keep going. You're doing great."

South First crossed Arnold Boulevard, then it turned into Steffens Street. The Civic was fun to drive. Very smooth and the engine had pretty decent power. Then I saw signs indicating that we were about to merge with Interstate 20.

"We want to go west, so just stay in this lane," Opa said.

I realized I was gripping the steering wheel tightly with both hands. "I've never driven on a highway before."

"Nothing to it."

"I don't think I should do this. I think I should pull over." Of course, by now, there *wasn't* any place to pull over.

"Bud, you're going to have to trust me. Just stay in your lane and go with the flow."

A big, black Ford truck was filling the rearview mirror, tailgating us. We took a ramp over the highway, then the ramp curled around and funneled us on to the interstate. Jesus. I was doing it. I was driving on I-20. Fortunately, traffic was light, but it was all moving at about seventy miles per hour. I'd never driven that fast before. The black Ford switched lanes and roared around me. I kept steady on the gas pedal.

"See?" Opa said. "It's not so hard."

I was too nervous to answer. I just kept driving.

We passed several exits, then several more. Before long, we weren't in Abilene anymore. Six more miles and the interstate skirted the small town of Merkel. Then I saw a sign that said it was nineteen miles to Sweetwater.

"How much further?" I asked.

"It's a ways yet."

An eighteen-wheeler was rumbling up beside me and I thought I was going to have a heart attack.

"Easy," Opa said. "Just focus on the lane in front of you.

He'll move on past." And, slowly, he did. I let my breath out. I was enjoying driving, but I'd had enough for now.

"Is your doctor in Sweetwater?" I asked.

Now Opa turned his head and looked at me. I could feel his eyes on me, but I had to watch the road.

"Not exactly," he said.

I was starting to wonder about something my dad had said yesterday — that Opa hadn't been thinking straight. "What are we doing, Opa? Where are we going?"

There was a long moment of silence. I wondered if he was going to answer me. Then he finally said, "I'm going to make you a promise right now, okay, Bud? That promise is, no matter what happens, I'm not going to lie to you. I never have and I never will. You're a young man now, and you deserve to be treated like one."

I had no idea what he was talking about.

But he wasn't done. He said, "So I will answer all of your questions as well as I can, with complete honesty, starting right now. 'Where are we going?' The answer is: Seattle."

I thought I'd misheard him at first. As far as I knew, there was only one city by that name.

"Seattle, Washington?" I said, thinking that couldn't possibly be right. I mean, come on, that would be crazy. Opa wouldn't just pick me up after school and take off across the country, especially without asking my parents. Would he?

"That's the one," Opa said. "We're going to Seattle, Washington."

Wondering how I felt? *OMG* doesn't even begin to cover it.

***

We turned north on Highway 84, taking us through Wastella, Inadale, Hermleigh, and Snyder, then through Brand, Dermott, and Fullerville.

What I didn't know was that by the time we reached Justiceburg — which was what my dad would call "a wide spot in the road" — my mom had already called my cell phone twice, leaving voicemail, wondering why I wasn't home yet.

I didn't get the messages until later because I still hadn't remembered to turn my phone on. Understandable, because one minute I was walking out the door of the school, the next I was driving Opa's Honda on an interstate highway. Not that I would've answered if my phone *had* been turned on. I couldn't imagine how anyone could talk on the phone and drive at the same time. Driving takes too much concentration. Heck, I couldn't imagine how anyone could *chew gum* and drive at the same time. Reaching for a stick of Juicy Fruit might be enough to send me careening off the pavement into a concrete embankment. That would be a stupid way to go.

I had a lot of questions, of course.

What's so special about this doctor in Seattle?

Why are you taking me along?

Why aren't we telling anyone where we're going?

On the other hand, I trusted Opa completely. I was sure he had a good reason for doing things this way. Besides, when it came down to it, this whole thing was pretty cool. Just ditching everything and taking off for Washington? What kind of pussy would turn down an adventure like that?

I'd ask my questions later. For now, I just kept driving.

"Welcome to Lubbock, Texas," Opa said, as we entered the city limits. "Flat, quiet, and boring, like the girl I took to my senior prom."

He looked over at me, grinning, so I grinned back.

People do make fun of Lubbock, but, so far, I didn't understand why. It looked like most of the west Texas cities I'd been to. A lot like Abilene, in fact. The only thing of interest that happened here was that Opa had me pull off the highway to fill up with gas.

He gave me a credit card to swipe through the gizmo on the pump, then he said he was going inside to take a leak. I noticed that he seemed to have some trouble getting out of the car, and when he walked toward the little convenience store, he was relying on his cane for support. I figured he was just a little stiff from being cooped up in the car.

I pumped the gas and got back in the Honda. Five minutes later, Opa still hadn't come out, so I moved to a parking spot in front of the store. I sat and waited, and that's when I finally remembered to turn my phone on.

At this point, it was nearly six o'clock — two and a half hours since Opa had picked me up at school. I figured my parents must be totally and completely freaking out, and boy, was I right.

I had seven voicemails from Mom. Yes, seven.

The first one: *Charlie, where are you? You were supposed to come home right after school. Give me a call when you get this.*

The second one: *Charlie, it's nearly four-thirty. Do I need to remind you that we're having dinner with Opa tonight?*

Well, I still was, but she wasn't. I wondered why parents always told you what time it was when they called. The time was listed right there on my phone.

The third message, only twenty minutes later: *Okay, it's official—I'm starting to worry. You need to call me immediately. Dad will be home soon and we're supposed to be at Opa's by five-thirty. Love you.*

Now I was starting to feel bad. She was sounding kind of desperate.

The fourth message, at five-fifteen: *Charlie...your dad and I are worried sick. He's driving around looking for you right now. You need to call back and let us know where you are. If*

you're mad about the talk we had in your room last night, I
apologize, okay? If you say you weren't in that house, then I
believe you. But you need to call me so I know you're okay.

Now I really felt like a major-league scumbag. I was about
to listen to the fifth message, wondering how much worse it
would get, when Opa came out of the store with a bulging
plastic sack hanging from his left hand.

He spotted me, came over to the car, and climbed into the
passenger seat. He seemed out of breath. "Hope you like
Gatorade," he said, pulling a bottle out of the bag, followed by
a bottle of water, a can of mixed nuts, several energy bars, and
a can of green spray paint. Weird.

"What's the paint for?" I asked.

"You'll see." He opened the can of nuts, grabbed a handful,
and then passed them to me. "Just a snack now. We'll stop
somewhere and get a decent dinner. You hungry?"

"Yeah, but we'd better call Mom first. I think she's going
crazy."

He didn't seem real concerned about that.

I probably haven't made this clear yet, but Mom and Opa
weren't the best of friends. Dad once explained it by saying
they had "philosophical differences," whatever that means. As
far as I could tell, most of it seemed to come down to Opa
voting for politicians Mom didn't like, and probably because
he never went to church. Not just our church, but any church.

Whenever we all got together, they spoke to each other
more like acquaintances than family members. Polite and
courteous, like when you see a neighbor at the grocery store.
They seemed to put up with each other, for the sake of everyone
else. When they'd hug — and Opa was a big hugger — there
didn't seem to be any real warmth to it.

So it didn't surprise me at all when Opa called Dad instead

of Mom. I only heard one side of the conversation, of course, and it went like this:

"Glen...No, I'm in my car...Yeah, I know...Because he's with me...Yes, right here...He's helping me run some errands... That's my fault. I should've called you earlier."

Then Opa listened for a very long time — maybe a full minute. Then he said, "Oh, for Christ's sake, that's absolutely ridiculous and you both know it...Ask me anything. Give me a math problem, or how about I tell you what I had for lunch yesterday? Think I can remember that far back? How about I quiz you instead and we'll see how well you do? What color was the tie you wore on Tuesday?"

What on earth were they talking about?

After another long wait, Opa said, "He's going to be fine. I just wanted to spend some time with him, that's all...No, you just need to relax...I'll have him home by ten o'clock...His phone is dead. The battery...No, ten o'clock. There's nothing to worry about....Okay, we'll see you then."

Then he hung up and let out a long sigh, the same kind of sigh dad lets out when he's getting tired of explaining something to me. Must run in the family.

We were still sitting in the parking lot at the convenience store, and I figured that was as far as we were going to get. No road trip to Seattle. I have to admit, I was a little disappointed. The big adventure was aborted before we'd even left the state.

Or so I thought.

Opa turned to me and said, "Let me ask you something, Bud. Are you concerned about my mental faculties?"

"What do you mean?"

"Do I seem senile to you? You know — losing my marbles? Be honest."

I thought about it. Yeah, this whole situation was unusual, but it seemed to me that Opa knew exactly what he was doing. So I said, "No more than usual."

I didn't intend it to be funny, but Opa laughed for a good, long time about that. Then he said, "Okay, then. Let's grab a burger somewhere then get back on the highway. We want to find Interstate 27 and go north."

5

It was amazing how quickly I'd become comfortable behind the wheel. I was starting to feel like an old pro. Driving really wasn't that difficult. Just stay in your lane. When you have to switch lanes, use your turn signal, and don't forget to check your blind spot. Don't tailgate. Don't drive too fast. Check your mirrors. Watch out for idiots. Those were the basics.

Even as the sun went down to our left and it began to get dark, it didn't bother me. It was fun driving by the headlights — or it was, until Opa said, "If a deer runs out in front of us, do *not* swerve, okay? And don't stomp the brakes. Just apply them firmly. Better to hit the deer than to lose control of the car."

"Okay."

"You have to think about these things ahead of time and already know how you're going to react. I swerved to miss a deer once and damn near killed myself. Hit a guard rail and tore up my car pretty good."

"What, this car?"

"No, it was a little Alfa Romeo I had a long time ago. I

wasn't much older than you. In my early twenties. I loved that car. You've never seen any pictures?"

"I don't think so."

"It was a red convertible. Man, what a car. I wish I still had it today."

I drove in silence for a few minutes, keeping the speedometer under sixty-five, which was the nighttime speed limit. Traffic was light, but occasionally a car would zoom past me going much faster than I was. A sign said that Amarillo was ninety-seven miles away.

"What happened to it?" I asked. "Your car."

He laughed. "You want the long version or the short version?" Before I could answer, he said, "I married your grandmother when I was twenty, right before I was sent to Vietnam. While I was gone, she loaned the Alfa to her brother, William. You never met him. He died in, what, 1977, I think. Anyway, he was driving the Alfa for a while, then he sold it. Wasn't his to sell, but he had a problem with gambling, so he sold it anyway. Irene didn't tell me any of this until I got back."

Irene was my grandmother. She lived in Maine and we didn't see her much. Once every few years.

"I bet you were pretty mad," I said.

"Well, yeah, a little. But mostly I was just glad to be alive."

I'd known that Opa had been to Vietnam, but I didn't know any of the details. He'd earned a medal of some kind, and he had some friends — other soldiers — that he met with every year or so.

Sometimes my dad would tell me that the world wasn't invented when I was born, meaning that a lot had happened before I came along. He would say he was young once, and so was Opa, and so on. But, honestly, it was hard to picture: Opa driving around in a sporty little convertible, then getting married so young, then fighting in a war in a country that I probably couldn't find right away on a map. It almost seemed like made-up stuff you'd see in an old movie, but I knew it was real.

"I blame it all on Joe Namath," Opa said, and I could tell from the tone of his voice that there was a grin on his face. "Super Bowl number three. Poor old William picked the Colts. Boy, that guy was the lousiest gambler. Had a talent for picking losers like you've never seen."

On the outskirts of Amarillo, Opa had me exit the highway and pull into the parking lot of a Motel 6. I found a spot in front of the office, and Opa climbed out of the car — slowly, using his cane for support — and went inside. I could see a young guy in there behind the counter.

I checked my phone and saw that it was nine-fifteen. Mom and Dad were expecting me to be home by ten o'clock. We wouldn't show, and my parents would start worrying again. I sure hoped Opa was going to call and tell them exactly what was happening.

A few minutes later, Opa came out of the office with a key and directed me to the rear of the building — the quiet side, he said, because it didn't face the highway. I grabbed his suitcase from the back of the car while he unlocked the door. The room was pretty basic: two queen beds, a TV, a small table, and a bathroom. Nothing fancy, but it was clean and functional.

"First thing tomorrow," Opa said, "we'll go shopping somewhere and get you some clothes, a toothbrush, things like that. Maybe buy an ice chest and fill it with some decent food, so we don't have to eat at restaurants three times a day."

"That sounds good."

He was still standing near the doorway. He glanced at his watch and said, "Listen, I guess I'd better call your dad and let him know what's going on. So I'm going to step outside for a few minutes. We'll have a little talk when I get back, okay?"

The "little talk" would turn out to be a conversation I'd remember almost word for word for the rest of my life, but I didn't know that at the time.

Here's something else I didn't know: Just as Opa was stepping out of the motel room, back home in Abilene, Matt was sneaking out of his house, carrying the stolen cordless drill in a brown grocery sack. He told me the whole story later, and it was a wild one.

See, Matt had what he thought was a great idea, but like many of his ideas, "great" turned out to be a really inaccurate description. What happened was, he had come up with a "strategic plan" to return the drill — but not to the house under construction. No, he figured that would be too risky, and I'll admit he was probably right.

After all, if the realtor, Cathy Abbott, had called the cops as my mother had urged her to do, there was a chance a patrol unit would be cruising past the empty house from time to time. There was also the possibility that the guy in charge of building the house — the contractor — had taken a few security precautions of his own. Maybe he'd installed motion-triggered security lights, or maybe he'd paid somebody to spend the night in the house, just to prevent anybody else from coming in.

So then Matt thought, *Well, if I don't return it to the house, how can I return it?* And he thought of Cathy Abbott. Matt figured it didn't matter where he returned it, as long as he returned it. And Cathy Abbott lived right in the neighborhood. So he decided to take it over to her house and quietly leave it on the front porch. She'd find it the next morning.

This is where I would've offered him a better option, if I'd been involved. I would've said, *Walk right up to her house with the evidence in your hand? Bad idea, dude.* Instead, why couldn't he just hide the drill somewhere near her house, then mail an anonymous note telling her where to find it?

But I wasn't there, so Matt formed his own plan, and just as he tiptoed onto Cathy Abbott's front porch, a car pulled into her driveway, and the headlights swept across Matt like he was an escapee in a prison yard. Matt dropped the brown grocery bag and ran, which, of course, made him look guilty of something.

The guy in the car, who turned out to be Cathy Abbott's large, fast, extremely strong boyfriend, sprang out of his vintage Firebird, gave chase, and tackled Matt before he'd even reached the end of the block. Did I mention that this guy had also been a state wrestling champion? He put Matt in a headlock and sort of half dragged and half carried him back to Cathy Abbott's house.

They quickly found the drill in the bag, and Matt had no choice but to tell them everything — everything except the fact that I'd been with him when he stole the drill. Even though it was kind of obvious I was his partner in crime — because, as we already know, Cathy Abbott had seen my big blond head through the kitchen window — Matt kept his mouth shut about that part. What he did say was that he regretted the whole thing, which was why he was returning the drill, and he was really sorry, and he wouldn't do it again, and that's when the boyfriend said, "I'm gonna call the cops."

They were in the living room and the boyfriend turned for the phone.

"Wait a second, Frank," said Cathy Abbott. "Just hold on. I mean, he *did* bring it back."

"Yeah, but he stole it first, and that was after they broke into the place."

Matt said, "We didn't break — "

"*You* shut up," Frank said, pointing a menacing finger. He was apparently a pretty wound-up guy. And he looked like he worked out with weights. Every day. For a couple of hours.

Matt shut up.

"Besides," Frank continued, "how do we know he was really returning it? For all we know, he was out there peeping through the windows, like a little pervert."

"Frank!" Cathy Abbott said. "For God's sake, if that was the case, why would he bring the drill with him?"

"Hell if I know. Maybe that way, if he got caught, he'd have an excuse. He could say, 'Hey, all I was doing was returning the drill.'"

It didn't help that Cathy Abbott was in a bathrobe and her hair was wet, apparently fresh out of the shower. Matt was shaking his head no, but he was too scared to speak up.

"That could be the silliest thing I've ever heard," Cathy Abbott said.

"But we don't *know* what he was doing out there," Frank said. "I think we should call the cops."

"Come on, Frank," Cathy Abbott said. "Remember when you were his age? Think about some of the things you did. We all make mistakes. I know I did, and you did, too. Let's not make a big deal out of this."

It sounded perfectly reasonable.

The jerk called the cops anyway.

I kissed a girl for the first time last summer, just a couple of weeks before my freshman year in high school. Matt and I were riding bikes one evening — not really going anywhere, just cruising the neighborhood — when we spotted Ashley, a girl from school, hanging out in the park with another girl we didn't recognize.

But man was she cute. Totally hot.

Matt, of course, had no problem riding right over and starting a conversation. He's always been confident like that, whereas I'm a little bit shy.

This other girl was named Tina, and she was Ashley's cousin from Dallas, just visiting for a week while her parents were on a cruise to Bermuda or the Bahamas or somewhere.

The girls invited us to follow them to the convenience store, where we bought some Cokes, and then we went back to Ashley's house and went for a swim in her pool. It was dark in the backyard, so Ashley's mom would occasionally stick her head out and check on us, but for the most part we had some privacy.

At first, the four of us talked as a group, but then we sort of broke into pairs, and Tina and I ended up on the other side of the pool, having our own conversation. Okay, not just a conversation. There was definitely some flirting going on, no doubt about it. She liked me, I could tell, and you can bet I liked her. She had a great sense of humor, and even though she was a cheerleader, she wasn't all snotty or stuck-up about it.

Still, even though things were going well, it took a *long* time for me to work up the courage to kiss her. I mean, it probably got to the point where she was thinking, *Jeez, what is this guy waiting for?*

But I finally did it. Just leaned right over, trying to be smooth, and kissed her. I'm not going to get all personal with the details, and what kind of kiss it was, and how many more times we kissed after that, but I will say that, the next day, I couldn't stop grinning. So much so that Dad finally nailed me. He said something like, "Any smile that big has to be about a girl."

I admitted that, yeah, I'd met someone. He didn't tease me too much, but he did get sort of philosophical or whatever and say that now, when I was young, through high school and college, I would have experiences that would stand out from all the others, and that I would come away with memories so strong and solid I could almost carry them in my pocket.

Corny, huh?

Turned out he was right.

I never saw Tina again, but even now, I can clearly remember the tone of her voice, the smell of her perfume, the exact green shade of her eyes. I remember that I had my arms around her waist and she whispered, "You're a pretty cool guy, Charlie," right before Ashley's mom came out and announced it was time for the girls to come inside.

What my dad hadn't mentioned was that it worked both ways. Some of those experiences and the memories they created wouldn't necessarily be good. Others would be downright painful.

6

After fifteen very long minutes, Opa came back into the motel room looking kind of shaken up or upset. I was sprawled out on one of the beds, channel surfing, and he sat on the edge of the other bed.

"I don't know what I was thinking," he said.

I sat up. "What? What's going on?"

He shook his head. "This was a bad idea from the start. I'm sorry. It's my fault."

"What did Dad say?"

Opa didn't answer right away, and when he did, it was a little hard to follow. He said, "I had no right to include you in this. Sometimes I forget that you're only fourteen. You're so smart, Bud, and you have a good mind, and I have no doubt you'll grow into a thoughtful, reasonable adult. But this is too much. Tomorrow, we'll go back home."

We sat there in silence for a long time.

The sports guy on the news was talking about the Longhorns baseball team, and how they could wrap up the conference title this weekend in the series against the Missouri Tigers. The coach, Augie Garrido, said, "It's ours to lose."

Weird, the things that stick in your head, even when you're not really paying attention. Even when you're wondering why everyone is talking in circles around you, without just coming right out and giving you the straight facts. Frankly, I was getting a little sick of it.

I was thinking about my parents, and how long it took them to tell me Opa was dying. According to what Dad told me in the car, they'd known since early April that Opa had cancer. But Dad hadn't told me until yesterday morning, almost two months later, when things had gotten so bad that he'd had no choice but to tell me. That didn't seem fair. Now I was wondering if Opa was doing the same thing.

"I deserve to know what this is about," I said, trying not to sound like I was whining or complaining. "You brought me all the way out here, saying we're going to see some doctor, but that's not the full story, I can see that. I'm not an idiot. You can say I'm too young to understand or whatever, but I think that's pretty lame. You've never treated me that way before. Everyone knows what's going on except me. Mom and Dad know. You know. I should know, too. I'm part of this family."

Missouri will have their ace sophomore pitcher on the mound for Friday night's opener, the sportscaster was saying. *So it should be a great defensive battle between —*

I turned the TV off.

Opa was looking at me and, very slowly, he began to smile. "You're absolutely right. It's patronizing. I'm sorry."

"You don't have to apologize. Just tell me what's going on. Please."

He took a deep breath. "Okay. Okay. I will. I could really use a drink of water first."

He started to get up, but I went to the sink and filled one of those plastic cups for him. He drank it all down and said, "Thank you."

"Want more?"

He shook his head.

I sat back down on the other bed, facing him. Our knees were almost touching.

He took another long breath, then said, "Let's talk about it — but let's do it rationally and logically. We're dealing with a problem that offers very few alternatives. Getting emotional about it won't help at all. There's a time for emotions — hell, I've got nothing against emotions — but there's also a time to set them aside and be pragmatic. Agreed?"

"That depends. What does *pragmatic* mean?"

He smiled again. "It means being practical. Some things you can't change, so you just have to deal with them and face the facts."

"Got it."

"Okay, first things first, let's just get this on the table: My cancer is terminal, which means I won't survive it. There's no question about that at all. I checked with a lot of doctors and they all said the same thing."

Already, I didn't like being pragmatic.

Opa continued. "So the next question is, what are my options? Unfortunately, there are only three. The first would be to do nothing. Let nature take its course. No chemo, no radiation, nothing."

"That doesn't sound like a very good choice."

"I agree. Which brings up the second option — follow the treatment plan the doctors recommended. It might give me a little extra time, but they've made it clear that my quality of life would be very poor. I would lose my independence and wind up in a hospital or in hospice care. Without going into detail, it would involve a lot of misery and suffering. Not just my own suffering, either, but your parents' suffering, and yours, too. I don't want that. Nobody deserves to go through that."

"But it's not up to you to decide what I'm willing to go

through." I wondered if I'd crossed the line. At home, Mom would've called that back talk.

But Opa said, "That is the wisest thing anyone has said to me in a long time. And, again, you're right. I realize that you'd be willing to endure quite a bit for me, Bud, and that means a lot. But I've decided I don't want to take that path. If that comes across as selfish, there's not much I can do about it. Can you understand why I wouldn't want to choose this option? Remember, we're being pragmatic."

I nodded, even though I didn't really want to. I *could* understand. It sounded horrible.

"Good," Opa said. "So that brings us to the third option. I can tell you right now that it isn't some magical solution that will make everything okay. You won't like it any more than the other two. In fact, you'll probably like it even less."

"What is it?"

"A way for me to have some control, to enjoy my final days with as much dignity and as little pain as possible."

"What is it?" I repeated.

He'd been fidgeting with the plastic cup, but now he set it down on the bed beside him and said, "It's called assisted suicide, Bud."

I don't know what I'd been expecting him to say. Not that, for sure. That idea hadn't even come close to crossing my mind. Never in a million years. Suicide? How was that an option? How could he even be considering it?

I must've had a pretty weird look on my face, because Opa said, "Sounds pretty scary, huh? So drastic. Maybe you even think it's a cowardly way out. If you do, I don't blame you. We're all raised to think it's a bad thing to do, and that's because it almost always *is* the wrong choice. Sometimes people get depressed to the point that they can't see any other alternatives. It's tragic and the people left behind are devastated. But this is a different situation. I'm not depressed — well, no more than you might expect. I'm angry, sure. I'm disappointed. I think about everything I'm going to miss and all the things I still wanted to do. We shouldn't talk about that too much, because we agreed to leave emotions out of it. We're looking at the facts objectively and realistically — just as I've been doing for the past two months. And the truth is, sometimes none of your choices in life are good. Sometimes you're faced with a terrible problem, and the only thing you can do is pick the least objectionable solution. Sucks, huh? Believe me, I wish I had a fourth option, or ten more options, but I don't. That's the only reason I'm even considering this."

Considering.

That picked up my spirits a little.

"So you haven't made up your mind yet?"

He started to speak, stopped, then said, "I honestly don't know what I'm going to do. This is new territory for me. I do know that nobody — not my family, not my neighbors, and especially not the government — has the right to make that choice for me. Ultimately, the decision is mine and mine alone, regardless of what I decide to do. And I know that I need to prepare myself now, not later, when my health begins to fail. That's what this trip is about."

"I don't understand."

"Assisted suicide is legal in only two states — Oregon and Washington. It isn't legal in Texas. No surprise there."

Now everything clicked. "So this doctor in Seattle isn't just a regular doctor."

"Well, she is, but her practice is limited to this one specialty — working with terminal patients who want to have a choice. See, it can get kind of complicated, legally speaking. There are a lot of hoops to jump through, forms to fill out. You have to talk to a second doctor — what they call a consulting physician. It's not as easy as, say, going to a doctor and getting an X-ray or a cholesterol test. And it shouldn't be. There's even a fifteen-day waiting period. The doctor can't write the prescription until fifteen days after your first request. I need to be up there, in Seattle, or this choice won't be available to me at all."

I didn't know what to say or how to react to all of this. I was even beginning to regret that I'd started the conversation. Just minutes ago, I'd felt mature enough to handle it — whatever "it" turned out to be — but now I wasn't so sure.

"I know this is a lot to take in," Opa said. "I didn't mean to just spring it on you like this. But after talking to your dad — well, he and I disagree on a lot of things, but I realized I was making you a part of my plan, whether you wanted to be or not. That was never my intention. All I wanted to do was spend some time with my favorite person in the world. That's you, Bud."

By now I had a huge lump in my throat, but I managed to control my emotions. I said, "So we're going home tomorrow?"

"That's the best thing, yes. It wasn't right for me to bring you along without telling you all the facts."

"Then what? You'll turn around and make the drive yourself?"

He shook his head. "No, I'll probably fly. Since you won't be with me, there won't be any reason to drive. Plus, well, driving across town is one thing, but up to Seattle? I don't think I'm up for that. A train might be nice. I haven't been on a train in a long time. Probably fifty years."

"But you're going, for sure?" I guess part of me was hoping that he wouldn't go through with it.

"Yes, Bud, I'm going. I would be lying if I said I hadn't made up my mind about that. But don't worry, we'll get to spend some more time together. Once I get settled in, you and your mom and dad can come up and visit. If you want to. It'll be beautiful up there in the summertime. You can go hiking in the mountains, go whitewater rafting, fishing. They've got a bunch of great museums, the zoo, the aquarium, the Space

Needle."

He was doing his best to sound optimistic and cheerful — trying to make Seattle sound like a fun vacation destination, instead of the place where he was going to die. I wasn't buying it and he knew it.

Opa stood carefully, without using his cane, then sat down on the bed beside me. He put one arm around my shoulder and pulled my head to his cheek, and I was about as sad as I've ever been in my life.

I didn't sleep well that night. At one point, I woke to the sound of Opa closing the bathroom door. He stayed in there for a long time, and after about ten minutes, I could hear him shaking an aspirin or Advil or something else out of a bottle.

The next time I opened my eyes, the room was much brighter, with light sneaking in around the curtains. The digital clock said it was fourteen minutes after seven. Opa was still in his bed, snoring loudly.

I could hear movement outside. Someone closing a car door and starting the engine, heading off to who knows where. Then I heard someone tromping on the floor of the room above us. Back and forth, from the bedroom to the bathroom, several times. Packing up, getting ready to leave. Maybe on vacation, or a traveling salesman, making a living. Just making a living.

That made me remember a time, at school, when we were talking about current events, and the teacher asked what each of us would do if we had a family — a wife or a husband and several kids — and we were running out of money. *What if you were about to wind up on the street, homeless, with no food, no money for any sort of emergency, desperate, nowhere to turn for help, and everybody you knew, all your friends, were in the same situation? What if all you had to do was cross a river, where lots of work was waiting? Even if it was illegal, if you had no other options whatsoever, wouldn't you cross the river? Wouldn't that be the right thing to do, for the sake of your family?*

They were rhetorical questions. She didn't expect anyone to answer, and nobody did. But we heard later that the teacher got in trouble for asking those questions. The rumor was that the principal told her to quit sharing her political opinions with students. Then he came to our classroom and gave his own speech, saying that there are always options, and that a man could always find work in his own country if he looked hard enough. The funny thing was, one student raised his hand and said, "My dad's been unemployed for a year and a half. How come he can't find any work?"

The principal's face got very red and he couldn't come up with a good answer. Weird. I don't know why I was thinking about that now.

I got up quietly and took a long shower. I thought about Mom and Dad, and it seemed like a week since I'd seen them last. I wondered if they were mad at me, and I figured they probably weren't. They were probably blaming Opa for this mess. But I wasn't.

After I toweled off and put yesterday's clothes back on, I noticed a brown prescription bottle on the vanity. The label said it contained something called hydrocodone. This was the bottle I'd heard Opa opening in the middle of the night.

I sat down on the rim of the bathtub, holding the prescription bottle in my hand. TAKE ONE TABLET EVERY SIX HOURS AS NEEDED FOR PAIN MANAGEMENT. MAY CAUSE DROWSINESS, DIZZINESS, BLURRED VISION, CONFUSION, OR LIGHTHEADEDNESS.

Opa has some wild ideas about what he should do next. He isn't thinking straight.

That's what Dad had said yesterday, after my driving lesson. But was it true? Were the pills to blame? I didn't think so. All things considered, Opa had seemed like his same old self last night. Just as sharp and logical as always. And braver than I could even imagine. It made me wonder what Dad would do if he were in Opa's place. I honestly didn't know the answer. I knew what Mom would do — and what she wouldn't do. No question about that.

What would I do? That was the most important question right now. Then I realized that's why I'd been thinking about that day in class. I probably couldn't figure out what I'd do if I were in Opa's place, but what would I do if I were the man on the other side of the river? Cross it? Or stay put and let my family suffer? Was there a right or wrong answer? Maybe there was an answer that was right for me, even if it might be wrong for someone else. I had a feeling Opa would think that was a pretty smart observation.

I put the prescription bottle back on the vanity, right where I'd found it, and opened the bathroom door. It was much cooler out here, away from the steam of the shower. Opa was still snoring. It was nearly eight o'clock. No more noise from the room above us.

I went to Opa's bedside and gently shook his shoulder.

"Opa."

He stirred a little but didn't wake up.

"Opa."

He moved a little more. His eyes didn't open, but he said, "Yes, what is it?"

"We'd better hit the road," I said. "It's a long way to Seattle."

7

In 1974, a millionaire named Stanley Marsh 3 halfway buried ten old Cadillacs nose first into an old wheat field. I swear I am not making this up. It's called Cadillac Ranch, and it's located a few miles west of Amarillo on Interstate 40, just off the historic old Route 66.

I didn't know any of this until Opa told me to exit the highway, make a U-turn, and go back east.

"Are you okay?" I asked.

"I want to show you something."

"What?"

"You'll see. It's pretty cool. Pull over right there."

"Where?"

"On the shoulder. There's plenty of room."

So I did. We got out and went through a gate in the fence, into a big, treeless field. No grass or weeds anywhere, just dirt.

"Aren't we trespassing?" I asked.

"No, it's okay. Follow me."

We started walking along a path — slowly, because Opa was using his cane — and then I saw them, several hundred yards away, in a perfect row. At first, I didn't even know what they were, because, really, who expects to find a bunch of old cars sticking up out of the ground in the middle of a field?

Then, as we got closer, I could tell that they were cars, and I could see that they were absolutely covered with graffiti. Top to bottom, people had painted every square inch of every car, even the wheels and tires and mufflers and oil pans, in every color you can imagine. Closer still, I could see names, dates, drawings, and just big swirls and splotches.

It might've been the strangest thing I'd ever seen in person.

"What *is* this?" I asked.

"Well, you could call it a roadside attraction, I guess, or a monument, or even an outdoor museum, but a lot of people say it's art."

"*This* is art?"

Opa grinned. "I'd say it qualifies. They call this sort of thing 'installation art.' It really is a sculpture of sorts, if you think about it. The man who owns this place hired a group of young artists from San Francisco to help him do it. He has a reputation for being a little wacky. The word they always use in newspaper articles is 'eccentric.'"

Funny, because that was the same word Mom sometimes used to describe Opa.

Then he told me a little about Stanley Marsh 3, who used a "3" at the end of his name because he thought the traditional "III" was too pretentious. Marsh came from a wealthy oil and gas family and had also owned some TV stations at one point.

"What some people say it's supposed to represent," Opa said, "is the golden age of the automobile. The oldest car here" — he pointed at one with his cane — "is from 1948. The newest one, that one over there, is from 1963."

"How do you know all this? Have you been here before?"

"Oh, maybe two dozen times. I stop by whenever I'm passing through. Actually, I've only been to this particular location a couple of times. It used to be set up in a different field, a mile or two closer to town, but they dug 'em all up and moved 'em out here about ten or fifteen years ago, to get away from urban sprawl. Part of the impact of the exhibit comes from the sheer isolation. Just a big expanse of nothingness — except for these cars."

We just stood there for a minute or two, taking it in. There wasn't anybody else around. I could hear the traffic on the highway, but it was much quieter than I would've expected.

Opa said, "See how they're all buried at the same angle to the ground? Supposedly, that corresponds to the angle of the Great Pyramid of Giza in Egypt."

"Is that supposed to mean something?"

"Well, I'm not sure. I'm not sure if it's even true. Could be just a rumor that got started somewhere."

He was wearing a light jacket, and now he reached into a cargo pocket and removed the can of spray paint he'd bought at the convenience store in Lubbock. He tossed it to me.

I gave the can a good shake, removed the cap, and approached the nearest Cadillac. The passenger-side door looked like a good canvas. In big green letters I wrote "OPA."

I should probably mention how Opa had reacted when I'd woken him up in the motel room that morning, before the Cadillac Ranch, and told him it was time to leave, because it was a long way to Seattle.

The first thing he said, after sitting up in bed, was, "No." He still felt it was wrong for him to take me along, but I kept arguing, and eventually he said, "You sure about this?"

"Yeah. You said you're going anyway. Why shouldn't I drive you?"

He hesitated. "I can tell you right now, your mom and dad

are going to be furious. But I'll take the heat."

"I'll take my own heat. This is my decision, not yours. I can handle it. Plus, as far as I'm concerned, they don't have anything to be mad about."

"Well, I am making you miss school."

"Yesterday was the last day. I'm all done. And I bet I got good grades, too."

Opa remained silent, thinking things through. I just sat there and let him do it.

Opa said, "We'll need to let your parents know. I don't want them to worry. They can be mad all they want, that's fine, but it wouldn't be fair to make them worry." He glanced at the little credenza by the TV, where he'd placed his cell phone and car keys. He let out a sigh. "This is not going to go well."

"Why don't we text them?" I said. "I'll do it. They'll probably feel better if they hear from me directly."

Opa nodded. "I think that's probably true."

I took my phone from my pocket. Mom or Dad? Dad, definitely. This is what I wrote:

Dad, im taking Opa to see a doctor, plz dont worry or be angry, everything is ok, having fun, will be gone several more days, will call later, love, Charlie

I showed the message to Opa.

"Looks good," he said.

I took a breath, then hit send.

We sat there, just waiting. We both knew what would happen. And it did. Less than a minute after I sent the message, my phone rang. Incoming call from Dad. It was hard to just let it ring and go to voicemail, but that's what I did. A tone let me know that he'd left a message. Then Opa's phone rang on the credenza. Then silence. Then a tone indicated that Opa had a new voicemail.

Then my phone rang again. Four times. Followed by a new voicemail.

"You know what?" Opa said. "I think we're gonna have to get us a couple of new phones."

And that's what we did.

Before we left Amarillo and visited the Cadillac Ranch, we stopped at a Best Buy and bought two new phones on a pay-as-you-go plan, then we went next door to an Academy and bought me a bunch of clothes, plus a cargo bag to carry it all. Now, less than two hours after seeing all those crazy upside-down Cadillacs, we were crossing the New Mexico state line and approaching a town called Tucumcari. Opa was driving, and doing a good job at it.

"I've heard of Tucumcari," I said as we passed the city limits sign. Population: 5,989.

"Yeah?" Opa said.

"It's in some song they play on Dad's oldies station. I didn't know where it was, though. That song is filled with a bunch of weird names."

We passed the Pony Soldier Motel and several small, flat-roofed buildings that looked abandoned, with weeds growing in the parking lots. A lot of the signs and buildings had an Indian feel to them, and the landscape was quite a bit different here. More rugged and rocky, with mesas in the distance.

Opa began to sing. "I've been from Tucson to Tucumcari... Tehachapi to Tonapah."

He looked at me and I laughed. His singing was horrible. "That's the one, but you're mangling it so bad I hardly recognize it. Can you sing solo?"

He frowned. "I *was* singing solo."

"No, I mean so low I can't hear you."

"Ha. You're just jealous that you didn't inherit my golden pipes."

"As if."

We passed the Dickinson Implement Company, Tee Pee Curios, an RV park, and even more motels. We stopped at a red light next to a restaurant with a gigantic adobe sombrero — like ten feet tall — over the front entrance.

"Bet they've got some pretty good breakfast tacos," Opa said. "Wanna give it a shot?"

I said that sounded good to me, so he pulled into the parking lot and we went inside. It wasn't very crowded so we got a table right away. Our waitress — a short, dark-haired woman with a broad, flat nose — came quickly with menus and glasses of ice water, then she returned a few minutes later and took our order. I asked for three breakfast tacos with chorizo, eggs, and cheese, plus a Coke. Opa ordered one taco, with egg and potato, and iced tea.

When she left, I looked around the room. There was a lot of corny artwork, with coyotes and eagles and cacti and that sort of thing. There were colorful blankets on display, hanging from wooden rods. It all seemed very old, like nothing had changed in here for fifty years, except for the flat-screen TV mounted on one wall.

The waitress brought our drinks. After she left, I said, "I like this place. It's different than the Mexican food restaurants back home. It's got more Indian stuff."

He said, "Usually they prefer 'Native American' or 'American Indian.'"

"Aren't I a native American?"

That made him grin, and I'm not sure why. "You sure are, Bud. Just not quite in the same way."

I started to ask another question, but I saw the waitress already coming back with our tacos. She put Opa's plate down first, then mine. Everything looked and smelled great, and I realized how hungry I was.

"Can I get you anything else?" the waitress asked.

"I think we're all set," Opa said.

She smiled, then went to check on some other customers.

I picked up one of my tacos and took a bite. It tasted great. And it was humongous. No way would I be able to finish all three. Maybe I could take one with me and put it in the ice chest. I wouldn't mind eating it cold in a few hours. I was about to take another bite when my eyes settled on the TV on the wall across the room.

And I froze with the taco halfway to my mouth.

At first, I was confused by what I was seeing. My mind just couldn't process it, I guess. It was so totally unexpected, like when you suddenly catch a glimpse of yourself in a mirror, except you didn't know there was a mirror there, so you don't understand for a second or two that the person you're seeing is *you*.

That's what was happening now, because there, on the TV screen, was a photo of me in my football uniform.

8

I didn't know this — again, this is something Matt told me later — but right about the time I was staring at the TV in disbelief, Matt was finally confessing that I'd been with him when he stole the drill. This was after he'd spent the night in jail. No, really. He spent the entire night, all by himself, in a holding cell at the police station.

What had happened was, Cathy Abbott's semi-Neanderthal boyfriend called the cops, so a patrolman came and questioned Matt, and then the cop called Matt's parents, who drove right over. Then there was a private discussion between Cathy Abbott, the cop, and Matt's parents, who were furious. Matt couldn't hear any of it, but he knew they were figuring out what to do with him.

Then the cop took Matt aside and said, "Miss Abbott doesn't want to press charges, but it's really not up to her, it's up to the guy who owns the drill. I'll talk to him later. But right now, I need to know something else. She says she saw someone with you at the house. Who was it?"

"Nobody. It was just me."

Honorable, I guess, but stupid.

The cop shook his head. "Come on, now. A tall, blond kid. I already have a name, but I want to hear it from you."

"I swear, I was all alone."

The cop sighed. "Let me tell you something. Your dad is mad enough to let you spend the night in jail. You don't come clean, that's probably where you're headed. I'd rather just get this cleared up right now, you know? We all know that your friend Charlie was with you. Miss Abbott went and talked to his parents yesterday morning."

Of course, Matt already knew that, and he knew that I'd denied everything, so he didn't want to make me out to be a liar. So he stuck to his story, that he was all alone. Brave, right? Well, he was, until the next morning. That's when a different cop — probably an investigator, because he was wearing regular clothes — told Matt they'd spoken to the man who owned the drill. Like Cathy Abbott, that man didn't want to press charges either — on one condition: Matt had to reveal who was with him that night.

"See, he wants your pal's parents to know what he did, so they can punish him," the cop said. "That seems fair enough, right? Letting the parents handle it? But if you don't give us the name, he's pressing charges. Against the both of you."

So Matt decided it was time to tell the truth.

It was my official player photo, the one they use for the programs they hand out at the football games. You know the type of photo I'm talking about — where the player kneels on one knee, with one hand resting on his helmet, which is on the grass next to him. So there I was, except they'd cropped in tight and all you could see was my face and the upper part of my jersey. Beneath the photo were two words: MISSING CHILD. The sound was down, so I couldn't hear what the announcer was saying.

I finally gathered my wits enough to put my taco down and say something.

"Opa." I was leaning across the table toward him.

"Hm?" His mouth was full.

"Opa, look."

"Look where?"

"Look at the TV." I was practically hissing.

He twisted and looked over his left shoulder. The photo was on the screen for just a few more seconds — long enough for Opa to know that I wasn't imagining things. Then it was gone, replaced by a commercial for a carpet-cleaning company.

Opa turned back around very slowly.

"Well," he said. Very calm about the situation.

"Did you see it?"

"I did."

"That was me!"

"I know it was, Bud. It appears your parents are, uh — "

"Overreacting?"

"Well, yeah, I'd say so. Was there a photo of me, too?"

"If there was, I didn't see it."

He glanced casually around the room at all of the other customers. "I don't think anybody here was paying attention."

I was getting past the initial surprise, and now I was getting angry. "It was my mom," I said. "It had to've been my mom. This is the sort of thing she'd do. She's a drama queen."

Opa didn't respond, but I could tell by the look on his face that he agreed with me.

"What're we gonna do?" I asked.

"I don't know yet," Opa said. "But for the moment, I'm going to sit right here and finish this taco."

I took over the driving duties when we left the restaurant. Opa had me stop at an ATM before we left Tucumcari. Then, once we were back on the interstate, he opened the glove compartment and took out a map of the western United States.

"There are several different ways to get to Seattle," Opa said. "And that works in our favor. They may think we're going through Colorado, Wyoming, Montana, Idaho, and over into Washington. Or we could be going New Mexico, Utah, Idaho, Washington. Or even New Mexico, Arizona, California, Oregon, Washington."

It was close to noon and the sunlight was pouring in at a steep angle through the windshield. Not a cloud in the sky. Traffic on the interstate was light. Opa had tuned the radio to an AM talk station coming from Albuquerque, thinking we might hear a news report about me. Or us. So far, it was just some guy ranting about the sorry state of our country, and how our liberties were being stripped away from us one by one. I didn't know what the heck he was talking about, but it sounded like he was about to have a nervous breakdown.

"Which way are we gonna go?" I asked.

"I was thinking we'd just wing it. Make it up as we go along. How does that sound?"

"Pretty good, actually."

He started folding the map. "In fact, the more unpredictable our route, the better."

"Because they'll be looking for us, huh?"

"Yep. Having second thoughts about this little expedition?"

"Not even a little bit."

"You can tell me if you are. I won't be mad."

"I would, but I'm not."

We drove without speaking for a couple of miles. The guy on the radio was still ranting, so Opa tuned it to a different station.

Something occurred to me. "Hey, how will they know we're going to Seattle?

"It might take them some time to figure out we're going to

Seattle, but they'll know we're going to the northwest. Remember what I told you in the motel room?"

Assisted suicide is legal in only two states — Oregon and Washington.

"Yeah."

"Plus, they'll know we went through Amarillo."

"Mom and Dad will know?"

"No, the police."

"How?"

"I used my credit card for the motel room."

"How quick — "

"And at Best Buy. And at Academy. And at the convenience store in Lubbock. We're leaving an electronic trail. That's why we stopped at the ATM. We needed some cash, and now we've got plenty. I withdrew the max with my debit card, then took out some more with my credit card. We'll pay cash from here on out."

I couldn't help but smile. Opa was pretty slick.

I asked, "How quickly can they figure out where you used your credit card?"

"I have no idea."

"On TV shows, they know that kind of stuff in just a couple of hours. And your phone records, too. They know who you called, and when, and where you were when you called them. You think they can get it done that fast in real life?"

"I just don't know, Bud. I hope not, but maybe."

I checked the rearview mirror, halfway expecting to see a police car zooming up behind us. But there was nobody back there.

I wish I'd been able to hear the news report at the restaurant. Were the police telling everybody where we were headed and which cities we'd already passed through? Did we need to ditch the interstates and start using smaller roads? We needed more information. My iPhone was in my cargo bag, along with my new clothes, but we couldn't use it. Not now. My new phone — the one from Best Buy — didn't allow Internet access. I thought about calling Matt and getting the scoop from him, but that would be risky. What if the cops were tracing his calls? Would they go that far?

Then I had a better idea.

The Moise Memorial Library in Santa Rosa was a small, one-story building made of brown brick. There were several parking spaces right in front, but I chose one to the far left, so the people inside couldn't see our car through the double glass doors. I'd bought a baseball cap at Academy; I put it on now to make my blond hair a little less noticeable.

"If they start asking questions, you get out of there," Opa said.

"I will."

"Try not to let anyone get a good look at your face."

I nodded.

"And don't hang out in there too long."

"Okay." He seemed to be done, so I said, "Be right back," and got out of the car. I realized I was having that feeling again — the one I had when Matt and I snuck into that empty house. On edge, but a little excited. Maybe even lightheaded. Like I was doing something I shouldn't, but there was a thrill to it.

I stepped inside and immediately saw several computers in carrels in the back of the room. Perfect. But first I had to get past the reception desk, which was occupied by a woman about my mother's age. She looked up from a book as I came through the door. No chance of slipping past her and sneaking onto one of the computers, because there wasn't a single other person in the library. Not one. So much for not letting anyone get a good look at my face.

"Morning," the woman said. She looked excited to see

somebody. Anybody.

"Hi."

"Can I help you with something?"

"Yeah, uh, yes, ma'am. I was hoping to use one of the computers."

"Sorry, they're all taken."

I didn't know what to say.

She laughed. "I'm just kidding. As you can see, you can have your pick. Kind of quiet around here this morning. I'll just need your library card."

I had assumed she'd ask that, because that's the way they do it at the library back home.

"Actually, I don't have one. I'm not from Santa Rosa. We're just driving through and I thought I'd stop in and check my email real quick. My phone quit working."

"Oh. Okay. Let's see."

She didn't know what to do, and she briefly looked around on her desk, as if there might be a form or manual somewhere that provided the answer. This was outside the normal procedures. I stood there.

She gave up looking. "Do you have a driver's license?"

"Not yet. I'm only fourteen."

"Do you at least live here in Guadalupe County?"

"No, ma'am."

I had a name ready, in case she asked for one. Dylan. I had always thought that was a cool name. So much better than Charlie.

"Where are you from?" she asked.

"St. Petersburg, Florida," I said, without missing a beat. Where in the world did that come from? I had no idea. But it wouldn't be smart to tell her I was from Abilene, in case she'd heard about a missing boy.

"Oh, I've been there!" she said. "What a lovely little town."

Just great. This was turning into small talk.

She continued, saying, "I loved that pier — the one with the building shaped like an inverted pyramid? What's that place called?"

"We just call it the pier."

"Well, that makes sense. We fed the pelicans. There were dozens of them!"

"They do like to be fed."

"One even climbed on top of our car."

"I hope it didn't scratch the paint."

"Well, with our car, you wouldn't even notice. Where are you headed?"

"Phoenix, Arizona. To see my aunt. She's having her spleen removed." I was really laying it on thick. It occurred to me that I was quickly developing the ability to lie effectively.

Now the librarian looked concerned. "They can do that?"

"Do what?"

"Remove your spleen?"

"Yeah, you can get by without it." I hoped that was true.

"That sounds serious. I hope she'll be okay."

"My dad says it's fairly routine surgery. She should be fine. But we're kind of in a hurry to get out there." Hint, hint. "My uncle is expecting us later tonight."

Now I wondered if that was realistic. How far was Phoenix from Santa Rosa, New Mexico? I didn't even know.

The library lady said, "Well, you're really supposed to have a card to use the computers, but you go right ahead." She said it with a smile, as if it would be our little secret.

I went straight to the web site for the *Abilene Reporter-News*, figuring they would be as well informed as anybody. There, listed third under the top stories, was a link that read: *Local man and grandson missing.*

My heart was beginning to race. This was so surreal. I clicked on the link and, when the page loaded, I saw two photos: one of Opa, probably from his driver's license, next to the shot of me in my football uniform. The article was short and to the point:

A 63-year-old west-side man and his 14-year-old grandson have been reported missing by the man's son, according to the Abilene Police Department. Henry Dunbar suffers from health problems and is on medication that might cause confusion. He is 5 feet 10 inches tall and weighs about 145 pounds, with gray hair and brown eyes. The grandson, Charles Dunbar, is 5 feet 11 inches tall and weighs 170 pounds, with blond hair and blue eyes. Investigators have reason to believe the pair could be headed toward Washington state or Oregon in a green Honda Civic. Anyone with information is asked to call the Abilene Police Department.

I glanced at the librarian, but she was at her desk, reading a book, so I read the article a second time. Could be worse. At least it didn't say anything about us having been in Lubbock or Amarillo. Then again, maybe the article hadn't been updated in a couple of hours.

The part about Opa's medications possibly causing confusion pissed me off. Okay, so it was true — the medication *did* have the potential to cause confusion. I knew that from reading the label. But Opa wasn't confused. I could vouch for that firsthand.

I did a quick Google search and checked a few other news sites, but none of them had any additional details. So I cleared the browser's history, logged off, and said a quick thank-you to the librarian as I hustled out the door.

Opa waited until I'd pulled away from the library and

gotten back on the road before he said, "And?"

I told him about the contents of the article — including the part about the medications. But instead of looking angry, he actually looked relieved.

He said, "To tell the truth, I was worried they might be treating it as an abduction."

"You mean, like a kidnapping?"

"More or less, yeah."

"But that's not what happened." I was amused by the idea that Opa could kidnap or abduct me, because I was bigger and younger and stronger than he was. And healthier. Plus, this was Opa, for crying out loud. He wouldn't abduct anyone.

He said, "I know that and you know that, but *they* don't know that."

"But I sent Mom and Dad that text message."

"For all they know, I could've sent that message myself from your phone. Regardless, it doesn't matter. If they want to think I'm some loopy old man, that's fine with me. That's probably for the best."

I stopped at a red light. "But it still doesn't completely make sense."

"Which part?"

"Well, if the cops think you're confused or loopy or whatever, but they know I'm with you, wouldn't they think I'd take you home or call Mom and Dad? Because that's exactly what I'd do if you were confused or loopy. But since I'm not doing that, isn't it sort of obvious that you know exactly what you're doing and that I'm helping you do it?"

He thought about that. The light changed and I pulled forward.

Opa said, "Here's a possibility. What if your parents didn't show the cops your text message?"

"Why wouldn't they?"

"I'm not saying they didn't — they probably did — but

I'm guessing the police would make the search a higher priority if they thought I'd coerced you into going with me. That text made it clear that you were doing it because you wanted to. The cops might not get too worked up about that. They might think it's a simple case of a kid going on a road trip with his grandfather, albeit against his parents' wishes. So they'd still take the complaint seriously, but it might not seem like such an urgent situation. Hey, pull in here for a second. Last stop, then we'll hit the road."

He was pointing at a small drugstore on the main street through Santa Rosa. I took a right into the parking lot.

"What do you need here?" I was hoping he wasn't going to fill a prescription, because that would leave another clue for the cops.

"You'll see."

I parked to the side of the building. Before I could offer to go inside for him, Opa was already opening his door, swinging his cane onto the pavement for support.

"Remember not to use your credit card," I said.

"Don't worry. Cash on the barrelhead."

"The what?"

"Never mind."

He was in and out in less than five minutes, holding a plastic sack as he got back in the car. He was grinning as he pulled his purchase from the sack. It was a battery-operated hair clipper or trimmer or whatever you call it. The thing the barber uses to give you a buzz cut.

"What's that for?" I asked.

Opa, still grinning, looked at the blond mop on my head. My most identifiable feature.

"Oh, you've got to be kidding me," I said.

Ben Rehder

9

It was getting late in the afternoon and Opa was sleeping in the passenger seat.

Meanwhile, I couldn't stop rubbing my head. It felt so weird with all of my hair gone. Well, not completely gone. It was maybe half an inch long now. About thirty minutes outside of Santa Rosa, we'd pulled into a rest stop along the interstate and Opa had sheared me like a sheep. It took about two minutes, tops.

Now, every few miles, I'd catch myself glancing in the rearview mirror just to see how different I looked. And it *was* a big change. If I were to walk up to Matt, it would probably take him a minute to figure out who I was, especially if I was wearing sunglasses and a hat.

Now it was nearly five hours since Santa Rosa and we had passed through Albuquerque, Grants, and Gallup, then crossed the state line into Arizona. Opa had been asleep for three solid hours, his seat tilted, his head back against the headrest.

He was sleeping so deeply, I was starting to wonder if he'd taken one of his pain pills when we were at the restaurant, or maybe when I'd gone inside the library. Not that I'd blame him. I'd broken my wrist when I was eleven — a compound fracture of both bones — and I knew something about pain. The funny thing was, breaking the arm didn't hurt as much as you'd think. It was a few weeks later, when the arm began to heal, that the pain really kicked in. It was a horrible throbbing that wouldn't let up. I remember that I had to take pills to get through the day, and especially at night, if I wanted to sleep at all. I don't know what the pills were, but I couldn't have gotten by without them. Mom doled them out every four hours, and not a minute sooner. She said she didn't want me "getting hooked." I didn't even know what that meant at the time. Now I wondered if the pain from my broken arm was anywhere as intense as the pain Opa was experiencing, or what he would experience later, as the days went by.

An eighteen-wheeler rumbled past and Opa finally began to stir. Just a little at first. Then his hand came up and wiped a bit of drool that had leaked from one corner of his mouth. He opened his eyes, adjusted his glasses, and sat up straighter in the seat.

"Where are we?"

"About an hour into Arizona. We passed a town called Holbrook about fifteen minutes ago."

"I need to take a leak."

I gestured backward with my thumb. "We just passed a sign that said Winslow is about twenty miles away."

I drove another mile and Opa said, "You're going to have to pull over. I can't hold it." He was sounding desperate.

"Here?"

There weren't any nearby trees to hide behind. The landscape was almost as flat as in west Texas, with just the slightest hills in the distance. There wasn't even any scrub brush, at least not the kind of stuff we called "scrub" back home. Here it was mostly just dirt and rocks and some wimpy little plants that weren't more than two feet tall.

"Yes, here, Charlie. Here."

I slowed and began to pull to the shoulder.

"Oh, hell," Opa said. "I'm pissing myself."

As soon as the Honda came to a stop, Opa had the door open and was getting out as quickly as he could, not even bothering with his cane. He stayed close to the car, one hand on the roof for support, and did his business. When he zipped up and turned around, there was a wet patch in the front of his pants. He looked at me. "Well, this is embarrassing."

I shrugged, doing my best to act like it was no big deal. "When you gotta go, you gotta go. You want to change pants?"

"Yeah." He looked toward the rear of the car. His suitcase was in the back.

"I'll get it." I hopped out of the car and opened the hatch. Then I looked through his suitcase and found a pair of khakis and some fresh underwear. When I came around the fender, Opa was trying to kick his shoes off. I knelt down, untied them, and slipped them off. Then I helped him put the clean clothes on, with Opa keeping one hand on my shoulder for balance. At one point, a car went past on the interstate and the smart-aleck driver honked his horn several times in rapid succession.

"You know," Opa said, "I've never been a very modest guy, but this is ridiculous."

We both laughed.

Opa buckled his belt, then held his arms out in a how-do-I-look gesture.

"Good as new," I said.

We both got back in the car and I eased back onto the highway. We were about a mile down the road when Opa said, "Bud, you are one hell of a grandson."

***

We continued on Interstate 40 through Winslow, Moqui, Dennison, Two Guns, and Winona. The sun was just setting by the time we reached the outskirts of Flagstaff, where Opa said, "I think we should grab a motel room. What do you think?"

"Yeah, I'm pretty tired, but I think we should get one a couple miles off the interstate."

"Probably a pretty good idea. Might as well look for one off Highway 180 going north."

"Why?"

"That's the way to the Grand Canyon."

"We're going to the Grand Canyon?"

"We're sure as hell not going to drive through Arizona and skip it. That'd be like going to Paris and skipping the Eiffel Tower. I don't believe you've ever been there, have you?"

"The Eiffel Tower?"

Opa laughed. "No, you big goof, the Grand Canyon."

"Uh-uh, but I've seen pictures."

He shook his head. "Pictures. Man, that's not even close to the same. Just you wait."

I'd just gotten out of the shower when Opa said, "Get in here, Bud!" It sounded urgent.

We'd stopped at a Dairy Queen drive-through for burgers, then found a motel on the north end of town. Not a chain, but what Opa called a "mom and pop" type of place, with very few cars in the lot. Like last night, in Amarillo, Opa went into the office while I stayed outside, in the dark, where nobody would see me. Opa paid with cash, but the manager asked for a credit card anyway. Opa said he didn't have one, because credit is a dangerous and predatory concept that devours the poor, and the manager finally gave in.

Now, thirty minutes later, Opa was calling out to me. I hate to say it, but my first thought was that he'd fallen down or something. But when I came out of the bathroom, tugging my shirt on, I saw that he was sitting at the foot of the bed, focused on the television.

And there it was again, for the third time. My football photo. I couldn't believe it. Why would a TV station in Flagstaff care about a small story all the way from Abilene? Didn't they have their own things to worry about?

Then I saw the logo down in the corner of the screen. CNN. I am not kidding. It wasn't just some local station, it was nationwide. Heck, even worldwide.

Now they were showing some other photos — from vacations and birthdays and holidays — photos that CNN obviously had gotten from my parents. Some shots of me. Some shots of Opa. Some shots of both of us together.

Meanwhile, the reporter was narrating: "...a rare form of bone cancer that is nearly always terminal. Henry Dunbar picked up his fourteen-year-old grandson Charles from school on Monday afternoon in Abilene, Texas, and the pair have not been seen since. Henry Dunbar's son, Glen Dunbar, told authorities that his father had recently been researching physician-assisted suicide, which is currently legal in only two states — Washington and Oregon."

Suddenly I was looking at my father's face in a video clip. He was standing at the end of our driveway, the house looming behind him. Judging by the shadows, it was shot late this afternoon, just two or three hours ago. The camera was zoomed in tight, so you mostly saw Dad, but I could see an arm of the person next to him. Mom's arm. Dad, looking somber, said, "We just want both of them to come home. My father is very sick right now, and a little desperate, and he needs the proper care. My son is really too young to understand this situation, and frankly we don't want him exposed to this sort of thing.

We don't support it at all. I want to make that clear. And that's not even really the point. My father didn't have our permission to take Charlie anywhere, and we want him back."

Now they cut to a second video clip — this one of a gray-haired man in a suit, standing outside a brick building. The reporter, narrating again, said, "According to Abilene police chief Walter Hoggins, there is an added wrinkle to the case."

The police chief said, "Charles Dunbar is alleged to have taken part in a burglary at a home under construction with one of his classmates this past Saturday."

I could feel my face growing warm. It was like a bad dream, when you show up at school in your underwear and everybody laughs at you. Very embarrassing. Now the whole world was going to think I was the kind of punk who steals things. Opa glanced at me quickly, looking puzzled, then returned his attention to the TV.

The police chief continued. "The charges against the classmate have been dropped, and we have no plans to pursue any charges against Charles Dunbar in that incident, but we think it might have contributed to his choice to flee with his grandfather. We have reason to believe they are on their way to the northwest. They could be in Colorado by now, or New Mexico, but we're fairly confident they are no longer in Texas. We will be working with other law enforcement agencies as necessary in other states."

Now they cut to a live shot of the CNN anchorwoman behind the desk in the studio. "Police Chief Hoggins later added that it was doubtful that any charges would be filed against Henry Dunbar, but that he needs to contact authorities as soon as possible."

She started on a different story, so Opa clicked the TV off. The room was suddenly quiet. Opa turned and looked at me. Crap. This was going to suck. I tried to stall the conversation by saying, "Well, at least they don't know exactly where we are. He said Colorado or New Mexico. And at least they didn't say anything about you being confused."

But Opa wasn't buying it. "Burglary, Charlie?" he said. Not *Bud. Charlie.* "What's that all about?"

"It wasn't really burglary."

"The police chief just said 'burglary.'"

"It was stupid. All Matt did was take a drill."

"From where?"

"A house under construction."

"How is that not burglary?"

I didn't have an answer.

"Did Matt own the drill?" Opa asked. There was something unique about his tone. He wasn't lecturing me. He wasn't angry. He was just asking questions.

"No, sir."

"Was he supposed to be in that house?"

"No."

"So he went into a house that he wasn't supposed to be in, and he took something that wasn't his. And you were with him? Inside the house?"

I nodded.

"Why?"

"Why what?"

"Why did you go inside the house?"

"I don't know. Dumb, I guess."

"No, that's the easy answer. Did you *want* to go inside the house?"

"Not really," I said.

"'Not really.' Does that mean a small part of you *did* want to go inside?"

"No. I didn't want to go inside at all."

"So why did you?"

"It was just a stupid mistake."

"Yeah, we know that. But that doesn't say why you did it."

"I guess not."

"Okay, then, walk me through it. How did it happen?"

This was getting painful. I didn't want Opa to think I was a thief.

"We were walking down the street and Matt saw that the door was open."

"Okay. Whose idea was it to go inside?"

"His." It felt good to blame it on Matt. He deserved it. It *was* his fault.

"You sure?"

"Absolutely. I tried to talk him out of it. I really did. I told him it was trespassing."

"But he didn't listen."

"No. He's stubborn."

"So then what? Why did you go with him? Why didn't you let him go alone?"

"I tried that, too. I told him to just go in without me."

"But he wouldn't do it, huh?"

"No."

"So how did he talk you into it?"

It was so ridiculous, so juvenile, so immature, I didn't even want to say it. But Opa was waiting. "He called me a pussy," I said. Then I added, "Not just once, but about ten times." As if that made a difference. "That's what he always does."

"Don't you think it would've been better if you'd just walked away?"

"Well, yeah."

"Was the police chief right about the other part? About that being a reason you came with me?"

"No way. I didn't even know the police knew about it. I even told Matt to return the drill to the realtor lady who came by our house."

I told Opa about the visit from Cathy Abbott, and how

Mom immediately suspected I was involved, and how Dad tried to step in, probably feeling sorry for me, because we'd just had that talk about Opa's condition. And, yeah, I even told Opa that I denied everything. I lied, in other words. But I wasn't going to lie to Opa, just as he'd promised that he'd never lie to me.

I said, "The whole thing was really stupid, and I knew it from the start. That's why I told Matt to return the drill. I figured if he did that, that would be the end of it. But I guess not."

Opa nodded and sat there for a few more seconds. Then he raised himself off the bed, patted me on the shoulder as he passed, and went into the bathroom. I heard the shower come on. It appeared our conversation was over.

10

My English teacher, Mr. Gardner, was always encouraging us to expand our vocabulary and use more expressive words. *Be colorful!* he'd say. *Paint a mental picture!* So here goes.

Stunning. Awe-inspiring. Intimidating. Jaw-dropping. Unbelievable. Rugged. Immense. Sensational. Breathtaking. Incredible. Astounding. Overwhelming. Epic.

The Grand Canyon was all of that and more. It was, without question, the most amazing sight I'd ever seen with my own eyes. Opa was right. Photos on the Internet couldn't even begin to compare. Not even videos. You had to see it firsthand.

We were standing at an observation station called Mather Point, which was right near the main entrance, not far from the visitor center. A trail ran in two directions from Mather Point to other points along the south rim of the canyon.

Before we'd gotten out of the car, I'd said, "Should we be doing this? Everybody's looking for us."

"Probably not, but we'll wear hats and sunglasses. It'll be fine. People aren't very observant. No way you're coming all the way to the Grand Canyon without getting the complete experience. Some things are worth the risk."

So here we were, just past ten in the morning and the weather was perfect. Not a cloud in the sky. The temperature was a little chilly, but we were both wearing jackets. And because it was a Wednesday, the crowd was sparse. That was lucky.

"Impressive, huh?" Opa said.

All I could do, for the moment, was nod my head.

"I first came here in 1959, when I was a kid. Your great-grandparents brought me here one summer. At that point, all those years ago, it was just a big ditch."

I grinned at his joke. I was glad he wasn't making me feel bad about the conversation we'd had last night, about the burglary. He hadn't even brought it up. We'd left the motel in Flagstaff bright and early, and it had taken about an hour to reach the Kaibab National Forest, then about another hour to reach the south rim of the canyon. When we'd first arrived, I'd wondered whether Opa could handle the walk from one of the parking lots to the viewing areas. Then he surprised me by popping the glove compartment and pulling out one of those disabled parking permits you hang from your rearview mirror. That made things easier. The walk was a little shorter.

"Check it out," Opa said now, pointing at a nearby sign. It said the Grand Canyon had something called a cell phone tour. Just dial a number from various points along the trail, enter a corresponding code, and you can hear a series of recorded two-minute messages from a park ranger.

"Give it a try," Opa said.

I whipped out my new cell phone — my first time to use it. I dialed the number and heard the voice of a man called Ranger David. He told me it was ten miles across to the north rim, that it was almost a mile down to the Colorado River at the bottom of the inner gorge, and that it had taken six million years for water to carve the canyon. He said that Arizona had once been covered entirely by a shallow sea. I hadn't known that. Or maybe I'd learned it and forgotten. Ranger David went on to say that the layer of rock that formed the "basement" of the canyon was 1.7 billion years old. If my mother were here, she'd be upset, because she was convinced that the Earth is only six thousand years old. It has to do with that part of the Bible with all the "begats," where you can trace Jesus' ancestry all the way back to Adam. If you add up all the years, from each generation to the next, you get about six thousand years. But that's not what we learned in science class, and that wasn't what Ranger David was telling me. I tended to side with Ranger David and the scientists.

The message ended and I hung up.

"That's pretty cool," I said. "You should try it."

Opa shrugged.

"You don't want to do it?" I asked.

Two older women, maybe retirees, were passing by on the trail behind us.

"Not really," Opa said.

"Why not?"

"Well, I don't want to sound like a braggart, but I already know everything there is to know about the Grand Canyon."

I heard one of the women giggle. Opa was showing off for them. He was using that tone of voice where you know he's kidding around. I was hoping he wouldn't draw any more attention to himself, but he kept going, tapping the side of his head with one finger and saying, "Every last fact, every last detail, right in here. Go ahead, quiz me."

The women had stopped about ten feet to Opa's left and were enjoying the view. They didn't seem to be paying attention to us, so that eased my nerves a bit. The hats and sunglasses were working, along with my short hair. Besides, who comes to the Grand Canyon expecting to see a couple of fugitives?

So I said, "Okay, you see the layer of rock at the very

bottom?"

"Yep," Opa said.

"How old is it?"

"Let's see. A little bit older than I am. Not quite two billion years old. One point seven, I believe."

What a smart aleck. And he was speaking louder than normal. Flirting with the old ladies.

"Lucky guess," I said, but I knew it wasn't luck. I looked past Opa, toward the women, and this time one of them was looking in our direction.

Opa said, "It's mostly granite at the bottom. Above that, you've got sandstone, and higher still, at the top, it's limestone, which is about 275 million years old. Shall I go on?"

I was trying to play it cool, but now both of the old ladies were looking at us. Not just looking, *studying*. I realized right then that they knew exactly who we were. They had seen the news reports. They had identified us.

"Opa," I said under my breath, but he didn't hear me.

"Here at the rim," he said, "we're at eight thousand feet above sea level. The river is about five thousand feet lower."

The ladies looked away, but they were only pretending to be interested in the canyon. It was obvious from the expressions on their faces. One of them snuck another quick sideways glance in our direction. I was starting to panic.

I leaned in close to Opa and spoke softly. "Play along," I said.

He looked at me, unsure what I was getting at, or maybe he hadn't heard what I'd told him.

"Okay, Uncle Joe," I said in a normal voice. "We'd better go. We're supposed to meet Danny at the car in five minutes."

For just an instant, I thought Opa wasn't going to understand the situation. He was going to blow it. He was going to say, *Danny? Who the hell is Danny?* And then the little old ladies would know they were right.

But what Opa actually said was, "And we know how cranky Danny gets when he has to wait."

Perfect.

We turned together and headed for the car. I fought the urge to hurry. I couldn't anyway, because Opa could only go so fast with his cane. He was moving along pretty good, though. Halfway to the car, I couldn't stand it anymore. I turned around, as if I wanted one last look at the canyon, and searched for the two ladies.

They were gone.

"Relax, Bud. Take it easy."

He was right. I was driving through the parking lot way too fast. Opa had his right hand on the door handle, bracing himself. But I wanted to get back on the highway as quickly as possible.

"They knew who we were, Opa!" I said. I had visions of park rangers pulling us over and putting us both in handcuffs. We'd get tossed into separate patrol cars and be hauled off to jail.

"You don't know that for sure."

"I could tell. They were looking right at us."

"Well, I'm a handsome guy. They couldn't help but stare. You shouldn't hold that against them."

I couldn't believe he was still kidding around at a time like this.

"They could be calling the police right now," I said.

Opa let out a sigh. "Yeah, okay, they could be. I don't think they are, but if you're right, there's not much we can do about it now. We might get caught, Bud, but we've known that all along, and I'm not going to let that ruin our time together. I don't want to keep looking over our shoulders every time we stop for a hamburger or check into a motel. If they find us, they find us. In the meantime, let's not worry about it. Okay?"

I eased up on the gas pedal. I took a deep breath. Maybe I'd overreacted.

"Okay," I said.

"Take a left here."

"Don't we want to go north?"

"We have to go east first. Have to go around the canyon, until they invent hovercars. We'll take this over to 89."

He didn't sound so hot. I looked over at him, and he seemed tense, like he couldn't quite relax back into his seat.

"You okay?" I asked.

"Yeah, I'm fine."

"You sure?"

"I pushed myself too hard. It wore me out."

I drove another mile. "Do you need your pain pills?" It was the first time we'd talked about it. He had to know that I knew about the pills — because, both nights, he'd left them right on the vanity in the motel room — but we hadn't discussed it.

Opa seemed to wrestle with the answer for minute, then he said, "Yeah, that would probably be best."

I parked on the shoulder, popped the hatch, and quickly found the prescription bottle in the suitcase. I got back in the car and opened the bottle.

"One?" I asked.

Opa nodded. He was unmistakably in pain.

I shook a pill into his hand and he swallowed it with some water from a bottle. "Thank you."

I swung the lid of the armrest upward, revealing the little storage compartment underneath. "I'll put them right in here."

He nodded again.

I had questions, but I didn't know if I should ask them or not. I decided I should.

"Do you feel it all the time?" I asked.

"The pain?"

"Yeah."

"No, not always. There are highs and lows. Sometimes I need to take something for it, sometimes I don't. Other times, it's just a sense of fatigue. No energy at all. But I might wake up the next morning feeling pretty good. I try to take advantage of those days. Unfortunately, the highs aren't quite as high as they used to be, and the lows are getting lower."

Thirty minutes later, he was fast asleep. Less than an hour after that, we came to Highway 89, just south of the little town of Cameron. I hadn't seen a cop yet, and now we'd be mingling with other traffic, not just vehicles coming and going from the canyon. I finally felt like I could breathe a sigh of relief.

While Opa continued to sleep, I followed 89 north up to Marble Canyon, where the highway made a big U-turn and headed southwest. I could tell the direction by a little electronic indicator on the dashboard. Southwest was no good. We didn't want to go southwest. I almost pulled over to study the map, but I didn't want to wake Opa, and eventually the road started going west. I figured west was okay. Northwest would be even better.

A little while later, we entered the Kaibab National Forest again. It was, in its ways, every bit as epic as the Grand Canyon, though I was still too rattled by our close call to come up with a long list of colorful adjectives. I remembered from looking at the map that morning that the forest surrounds the canyon on both sides. So now we were north of the canyon, which meant I was on the right track.

We crossed into Utah and made it to Salt Lake City about an hour after sundown. Earlier in the afternoon, Opa had woken after several hours of sleep, and I could tell he was still very uncomfortable. I'd recommended stopping for the day at one of the smaller towns we'd passed through — Kanab or Cedar City or Parowan — but he'd said no, he wanted to keep moving.

We'd also had a conversation about our route: Stick to the interstates or take smaller highways? Or did it even matter at this point? The cops might be looking for us on the interstates. On the other hand, if they thought we were smart enough to know they would be looking for us on the interstates, then we might take the smaller roads, so they'd look for us there. In the end, we figured they were probably looking for us everywhere, so we decided we should just take whatever route we wanted to take. It was a lot easier that way.

We did the same thing we'd done last night: Found a mom-and-pop motel and Opa managed to check in without a credit card. I guess he has a face that people trust. I know I trust him.

Opa was sleeping again.

I was in bed, lights out, switching back and forth between the major national news channels. If you'd told me a week ago that I'd be watching CNN and MSNBC on a nightly basis, I'd have said you were on crack.

But I wanted to know what was happening. If those ladies had really recognized us at the Grand Canyon, it would probably make the news. Or, heck, I guess there was the chance that we were already old news. Maybe we'd already been bumped from the headlines by bigger stories. I watched for an hour and didn't see anything about us.

I woke sometime later and the TV was still on. Lying there, drowsy, I thought I heard Opa's name. Then I heard it again. I sat up, now wide awake. There was an older man on the screen, apparently in the middle of answering a question.

"...and it is, of course, a very divisive issue, but this situation with Henry Dunbar emphasizes how important it is for terminally ill patients to have the right to die with dignity. These ridiculous laws should be struck down and assisted suicide should be an option in all fifty states. It's astounding to me that the government thinks it's their job to intrude on Mr. Dunbar's life and make healthcare decisions for him. Just as they can't force an adult to accept treatment, they shouldn't presume to have the power to deny this option."

Now the screen split, revealing a younger woman in a different location. This wasn't just an interview, it was a debate. I thought about waking Opa, but I decided against it. Better to let him sleep.

The young woman said, "As you can imagine, I disagree with that entirely. Assisted suicide is a vulgar cheapening of life and it goes against everything the medical establishment stands for. Doctors are supposed to help people, not kill them."

The man attempted to say something, but the woman kept going.

"These laws are in place to protect people with disabilities, people with depression, and those sorts of things, because those are the types of people that would be victimized the most by assisted suicide. It truly is appalling, because we should be offering them the resources and solutions to deal with their health problems, not putting them to sleep like the family dog. And how long will it be before we start prescribing suicide for people who haven't asked for it, simply because it's the cheap and easy way out? Morbid is the only word that describes it adequately."

The man was shaking his head vigorously. The interviewer, off screen, said, "Jack, I'll let you have the last word."

The older man said, "Rachel is building an enormous straw-man argument and I'm pretty sure she knows that. Nobody is suggesting that assisted suicide is appropriate for people with treatable conditions such as depression, and the idea that assisted suicide would ever be forced on anyone is a total misrepresentation. That wouldn't be suicide, that would be murder, and I don't know anybody who would ever support that. To the contrary, assisted suicide gives real human beings the ability to die with peace, rather than with needless pain and suffering. It allows individuals who are facing certain death to take some control and end their lives on their own terms, and I think that is the most compassionate thing we can offer them. Henry Dunbar is forcing all Americans to come to terms with this issue, and in my view that makes him a true hero."

11

I guess I was pretty tired from all the traveling, because I slept until nearly nine o'clock. First thing I did when I woke up was look over at Opa's bed. He was still asleep. No snoring this time. The TV screen was dark, so he must've gotten up sometime during the night and turned it off.

I settled back into the pillows.

What day was today? I'd lost track. Opa had picked me up at school on Monday, then we'd stayed one night each in Amarillo, Flagstaff, and now Salt Lake City. So today was Thursday.

On most weekday mornings, Dad would be at work by now, assuming he was still going in each day, instead of waiting around for me to come home. Mom, if she was following her routine, would be working out at the gym, and then she'd stop at the grocery store to pick up some things for dinner.

More likely, though, she was sitting in front of the TV, watching the same news channels I'd been watching, hoping for some new bit of information about her baby. Probably with a box of Kleenex on the table beside her. She can be pretty melodramatic that way. But, I have to admit, lying there in bed, I began to feel ashamed for what I was putting my parents through. I knew — and I'd known from the beginning — that I was letting them down. Even though I felt I was doing the right thing, I was still disappointing them, which really sucks, if you think about it.

The truth was, I missed them both a lot. And Matt, too, and all my other friends. I was a little bit homesick. I wanted to grab my phone and let all of them know everything was fine. There was no reason to worry. Even tell them I was sorry. It would mean a lot to hear Mom's voice. It really would.

For the first few minutes, anyway. I could picture how the conversation would go. She'd be so sweet and happy and, well, motherly, at first. But that would slowly change. She'd start to chastise me for doing what I'd done. Then she'd start to say angry things about Opa.

Why was I thinking about this? What purpose did it serve? All it did was stress me out. Besides, I'd already made my choice.

I woke up for a second time. Now it was ten-fifteen. Opa's bed was empty. I waited, expecting to hear water running in the bathroom, or just the sound of him moving around.

Nothing.

Several minutes passed.

Then I heard an unmistakable sound. Opa was throwing up. I got out of bed and approached the closed bathroom door.

"Opa?"

"Yeah?" His voice was weak.

"You okay?"

"Can you do me a favor?" It barely sounded like him.

"Yeah, sure."

"I think my pills are out in the car."

That's right. I'd put them in the little storage compartment under the armrest.

"I'll go get them."

"Thank you."

"Need anything else?"

"Just the pills."

"Be right back."

I quickly pulled on my shorts, a shirt, and my sneakers, then grabbed the room key and the car keys off the credenza. I stepped outside and found myself looking at mountaintops in the distance. We'd gotten in too late last night for me to get a good look. Now they stretched across the horizon, set sharply against the blue sky, with snow still visible on some of the peaks. I didn't know which mountains they were, but they were pretty awesome.

Our room was set back from the parking lot, so I had to walk past the small fenced-in pool to get to the car. The weather was incredible. Warm, but not hot. The air was dry. Back home, it would probably be one hundred degrees by mid-afternoon.

I stepped off the curb beside Opa's Honda and came to an immediate stop, because something was wrong. Majorly wrong. Horribly, unthinkably wrong.

The driver's side door was open.

Not all the way. Just a few inches. But it was open. Either I'd forgotten to close it last night, which didn't seem likely at all, or someone had been inside the car. A thief had been inside the car.

I looked around the parking lot. Nobody. Just a couple dozen cars and trucks scattered here and there. None of their doors were open.

My gut told me this wasn't going to end well. There was very little of value inside the car. My bike was still in the back. I'd taken most of our other things inside last night — but not the pills. I had forgotten about them.

I eased the car door all the way open and slid into the driver's seat. The glove compartment was open, and I didn't see Opa's handicapped parking permit, so I had my answer. Somebody *had* been inside the car. Then I realized my new cell phone was also gone. I'd left it out here, because there was no reason to keep it on me. Not like anyone was going to be calling me. But the loss of those two items didn't bother me. In the scheme of things, they weren't important.

Now I hesitated. *Please God. Let Opa's medicine be there.* I lifted the armrest cover so I could check underneath. I really didn't even want to look, but I finally did.

The storage compartment was empty.

The goddamn prescription bottle was gone.

"Hey!"

It took me a couple of seconds to locate the person who had just called out. Then I spotted her on the far side of the pool — a girl in a lounge chair, stretched out just as comfy as you please. Wearing a red bikini top, white shorts, and flip-flops. Plus sunglasses with red frames, and a floppy straw hat with a wide brim. A magazine was lying across her thighs. I hadn't noticed her on the way out, but only because I hadn't glanced that direction. Believe me, if I *had* glanced that direction, I would have noticed her. She gestured with her arm, like *Come over here*, so I walked over to the fence.

Before I could say anything, she said, "That your car?" Apparently she could see the parking lot from where she was sitting, even with the sun caressing her skin the way it was.

"Yeah," I said, because I'm such a skilled conversationalist.

"Anything get stolen?" she asked.

"Yeah. How did you know?"

"I saw the guy that did it."

"When?"

"About thirty minutes ago. I was watching him, but he didn't see me. He's long gone."

"Well, Jesus, why didn't you do anything?"

Suddenly, like I'd flipped a switch, she looked pissed. "Because I didn't know it wasn't his car, genius." A real snotty tone. "Not until after he left."

I held up my hands. "Okay. You're right. I apologize."

That seemed to satisfy her. "So what'd he take?"

I shook my head. "My grandfather's medicine."

She wrinkled her nose. I have to mention that it was a very cute nose. I could see some blond hair poking out from underneath her hat. "Why would he want that? What kind of medicine?"

"Just, you know, medicine. Look, I have to go. Thanks for letting me know what happened."

She shrugged and went back to her magazine.

He was back in bed. His eyes were shut, but I could tell he was awake. He had the blanket pulled up tight to his chin. It was very cold in the room. He'd turned the AC down. I sat down on the edge of my bed.

"Opa?"

"Yeah, Bud."

"I think I really screwed up last night. Something bad happened and it's all my fault."

His eyes opened. "What's wrong?"

I didn't want to say it, but I finally did. "I left the car unlocked. Some guy got inside and took your medicine."

I wish I hadn't seen what I saw next, but an expression flashed across Opa's face before he could stop himself. It was a look of desperation. A look that said, *What the hell am I going to do now?* I can't tell you how incredibly stupid and irresponsible it made me feel. Burglarizing that empty house with Matt — and having that fact broadcast on national TV — was nothing compared to this. Letting him down like this was as bad as it gets.

"He took the parking pass, too," I said. "And my phone. A girl at the pool saw it happen, but she didn't know it wasn't his car, so she didn't stop him. I'm really sorry."

He shook his head a little. "Not your fault."

"Yeah, it was. If I'd locked the doors..."

"Stop it. These things happen, Bud."

I didn't know what else to say. What an idiot. Imbecile. Moron.

Opa said, "I think I might have one pill stashed away in my shaving kit. Would you check?"

I did, and he was right. One last pill. Better than nothing, but not nearly enough. I brought it to him, along with a glass of water. Even swallowing seemed to cause him some discomfort, and now he'd have to face it without any medicine, thanks to me.

But I was about to feel even worse, if that was possible, because Opa said, "You know, maybe this is for the best. I've been doing some thinking."

"About what?"

"Well, I think maybe we've reached the end of the road."

"What are you talking about?"

He took a deep breath and slowly let it out. "I never meant for you to see me like this. I thought I could hold out longer, until we reached Seattle. But this is too much. I can't ask you to do this anymore."

Once again, like in the car with Dad on Sunday, and in the Amarillo motel room with Opa, my eyes were beginning to water. "But we're more than halfway there," I said. "If we get a real early start tomorrow morning, we could be there late tomorrow night." But even I could hear the defeat in my voice.

It was over, and I knew it. Opa didn't want me to see him in misery, and even though I knew I could handle it, I shouldn't have been asking him to keep going. What kind of selfish jerk does something like that?

"We got a chance to spend some time together," he said, giving me a weak smile. "That's the important thing. And it meant a lot to me. You're the best traveling buddy I've ever had."

Hot tears were streaming down my cheeks. It seemed like I'd cried more this week than I'd cried in my whole life. I didn't care. If this wasn't a good reason to bawl like a little kid, what was?

"What're we gonna do?" I asked, wiping my eyes with the back of my hand. "Call Mom and Dad?"

But Opa was already drifting off again.

12

"Hey!"

It was her. I'd come back outside, because I didn't know what else to do. I didn't want to stay cooped up in the freezing motel room. Now the blond girl by the pool was waving me over again. Kind of pushy. I walked over to the fence. It was even warmer now than it had been just twenty minutes ago. I'd left my sunglasses inside, so I was squinting. That was fine, because it would prevent her from seeing my red eyes.

"What'd he say?" she asked.

"Who? My grandfather?"

"Yeah. Are you in trouble?"

It was an unexpected question. In trouble? With Opa? I couldn't remember ever getting in trouble with Opa. He wasn't the kind of grandfather who ever made you feel like you were in trouble. "Not really."

"Is he gonna call the cops?"

"No."

"Why not?"

"You said it yourself. The guy's long gone."

She nodded, as if she were agreeing that she was pretty

wise. Then she stopped nodding, but was still staring at me. "So are you gonna go swimming or what? Come join me. I'm bored."

I can tell you this much: If a girl like that had invited me swimming at any other time, I would've been doing back flips. Not literally, but you know what I mean. It would have made my day.

"I don't have a swimsuit." She must've thought I was a real loser. How often does a hot girl like her invite a guy like me to go swimming?

She said, "Who cares? Swim in your shorts."

I was going to say no. I mean, sure, I was tempted. But it just seemed wrong, under the circumstances. I shouldn't be out here having fun, right? But then she sat up, took off her hat, and removed a clasp that was holding up her hair. Remember Mr. Gardner, my English teacher? If I were describing this scene in a paper, he'd want me to find just the right verb for what this girl's hair did. And that word would be —

Cascaded.

Yep. No better way to describe it. Her long, wavy, blond hair cascaded over her shoulders and down her back. She looked like a model in a shampoo commercial.

I opened the gate and followed the concrete apron around the pool. I sat down on the lounge chair next to hers. Up close like this, she was even prettier than I had first thought. Like prom queen kind of pretty.

"What's your name?" she asked. Now she was messing around with her iPhone. I hoped she wasn't one of those girls who sends a text every thirty seconds. That drives me crazy.

"Dylan."

"Where are you from?" Not looking at me. Still busy with her phone. Kind of rude.

"St. Petersburg, Florida," I said. Same thing I'd told the librarian in Santa Rosa. Might as well be consistent.

"What are you doing in Salt Lake?"

What was this, a pop quiz?

"On our way to see a sick aunt. She's having her spleen — "

"Ha! I knew it!"

She suddenly held her phone up and showed me the screen. She hadn't been sending a text at all. She'd been surfing the web. Logging on to CNN. On her phone was that same old photo of me in my football uniform. "Dylan, my ass," she said. "You are totally busted." She was grinning, like she'd solved some big mystery. Proud of herself for being clever.

I just sat there. What the hell else could I do? She'd nailed me. That's why she'd invited me over. To get a closer look. And there was no point in freaking out about it anyway, was there? Not since Opa had decided it was time to call it quits.

"Well, that's not the reaction I was expecting at all," the girl said, wrinkling her nose. "This *is* you, right?"

"Yeah." Why deny it?

"Aren't you worried I'm gonna turn you in?"

"Not really."

She gave me a funny look, then lowered the phone. "It's Michele, by the way. My name."

"I'm Charlie."

"Well, duh. Charlie Dunbar, from Abilene, Texas. Everybody's looking for you."

"I know. I've seen the news."

"You cut your hair."

"Opa did it."

"What's an opa?"

"That's what we call him. My grandfather. Opa."

She tilted her head, studying my hair. "It looks good like that."

"Thanks. But you still recognized me."

"I'm very observant. Plus, the Honda was a giveaway. Texas license plates and everything. I'm surprised nobody has spotted you guys yet. You're all over the Internet. Here, check this out." She tapped some more keys on her phone, found what she was looking for, then passed it to me.

The screen showed a Facebook fan page. It was called *Let Charlie and his grandpa make it to Seattle.*

"You see how many fans you've got?" Michele asked.

I couldn't believe it. The total was 963,277. Nearly a million people. I started reading some of the comments.

Charlie and his g-pa are awesome!

The government should butt out. It's none of their business!

So cool, it shd b a movie.

This is a very touching story and I hope it ends as well as possible. Godspeed Charlie Dunbar.

I scrolled down. There were more comments. Lots more. Thousands in just a few days. People from across the country and around the world were throwing their support behind Opa and me. It was really amazing. These total strangers wanted us to complete our journey. The bummer was, we were going to let all of them down. Well, I was, not Opa. I gave the phone back to her.

"Pretty awesome," I said.

"Then why do you look like someone just ran over your puppy?"

This Michele was a character, as my mom would say.

"We're not going to make it to Seattle," I said.

"Why not? I'm not going to tell anybody. You were right not to be worried about that, because I think what you're doing is way epic."

"Thanks."

"So what's the problem?"

I shook my head. "Long story."

She snorted. "Summer break just started, Chuck. Anyone ever call you Chuck? I've got nothing but time."

I could tell that Michele was the kind of girl who probably

got all the answers she wanted — not just because of her looks, but because she was funny and easy to talk to. So I talked. I told her some details about Opa's condition, and that he was in a lot of pain, and that he had to take medicine to make it manageable.

"Let me guess," she said. "That was the medicine that jerk stole from your car."

"Yep."

"Major suckage."

"Yep."

"And it's not like your grandpa can just call the local Walgreen's for a refill."

"Nope."

Then she got this odd look on her face. Like an idea had popped into her head. "Whoa," she said.

"What?" I asked.

"I just thought of something."

I waited.

"I might have the answer," she said.

"Are you going to tell me, or do I have to pry it out of you?" I was losing my patience.

She grinned again. Not a smile, definitely a grin. Mischievous. "You're gonna love me, Chuck. You're gonna think I'm the greatest girl on the planet."

"I — "

"You know what a prolapsed disc is?"

"Not really."

"Well, my dad sure does."

The next thing I learned — after Michele told me that her father, who worked in a warehouse, had been dealing with a lower-back injury for more than eight years — was that she lived about a block away.

It turned out she wasn't a tourist, she simply liked to use the motel pool because it was close to her house. She swam there whenever she wanted. The manager didn't seem to care, as long as she didn't get rowdy or bring more than one friend at a time. Preferably another pretty girl, the manager had told her. "He's a little creepy, but basically harmless," Michele said.

Now we were walking up the steps to her house. It was a small brick house, but it looked okay. The lawn was mowed and all that stuff.

"My dad is at work and my mom is shopping," Michele said, unlocking the front door.

That helped me relax a little, but the situation still reminded me of the disaster with Matt and the empty house. I felt like I wasn't supposed to be here. We stepped inside and Michele closed the door behind us.

"Got any brothers or sisters?" I asked, because I didn't want any surprises.

"Just Tim. He's away at BYU."

"What's that?"

"You don't have to whisper. There's nobody here. You've never heard of BYU?"

"I don't think so."

"The Mormon college in Provo?"

"Oh, Brigham Young. You're Mormon?"

"I guess. Well, my parents are, sorta. I guess that makes me one, too, doesn't it?"

I thought that was a strange way to look at it, but I didn't say anything. I especially didn't mention that my mom wouldn't approve of me hanging around with a Mormon. Mormons were almost as bad as atheists.

Michele dropped her keys and phone on a little table and proceeded down a hallway to the left. I followed her. I wanted to get back to the motel quickly, even though I'd gone back into the room and left a note for Opa before we left. I'd told him not to call anyone, because I might have a solution, and I'd tell him more when I got back.

"My parents' room is back here."

She turned into a room on the right and flipped the light on. The room was nice and neat, with the bed made. But it wasn't like she was giving me a tour. She went straight into the bathroom and started opening some drawers under the vanity. She found a brown prescription bottle, checked the label, then put it back. Then did the same thing with another one.

"I know he'll have some pills around here somewhere. My mom insists on keeping some around, because when his back gives him trouble, he can be a real you-know-what."

I would only need a few pills. Just two or three. Enough to get Opa to Seattle. And if there were enough pills in the bottle, Michele's dad might not notice that any were missing, so she wouldn't get into trouble.

She opened another drawer. No prescriptions there. The bottom drawer. Nothing. The medicine cabinet. Zilch. I was amazed at how boldly she was rooting around in her parents' stuff. She didn't even seem all that concerned with putting everything back just the way it was. She exited the bathroom and went to the nightstand on the right side of the bed. Only one drawer to explore. No medicine. She circled to the nightstand on the other side. Goose egg.

"Well, fudge," she said. She had her hands on her hips and her bottom lip stuck out, thinking. It was very cute. She was still wearing her bikini top and those white shorts. I was having a tough time keeping my eyes off of her. And she caught me. She caught me checking out various parts that I shouldn't have been looking at. Wait, that's not exactly true. It's only natural to look at those parts, but it's smart to show a little discretion. That means be respectful and only sneak a peek when you can get away with it. Don't ogle, which is what I was doing before I finally looked up and —

She'd been watching me. She knew where my eyes had been. Still, she smiled. Her dimples were spectacular.

"Hey, guy. I need you to focus," she said.

I *had* been focusing. That was the problem.

"It's okay if you can't find them," I said.

"I'm not giving up yet."

And she didn't. She searched the kitchen, the guest bathroom, the living room, her brother's old room, even the garage. I just followed her around, hoping she'd have some luck. But it was obvious that she was running out of places to look. And I was wishing that I hadn't said anything promising in the note I'd left for Opa.

Finally, she plopped down on the couch in the living room and I did the same.

"I'm really sorry, Chuck."

"Don't worry about it. It was a good idea. Thanks for trying."

"I know they're here somewhere, I just don't know where."

"It's okay."

"You know, I think it's really sweet what you're doing for your grandfather. For your Opa. I wish I could help."

She turned her head toward me, then put her hand on the couch between us with her palm upward. It was obvious what she wanted. I reached out and clasped her hand in mine. I could feel my heart beating heavily. Something good was about to happen. It reminded me of last summer, in the pool, with that other girl whose name I couldn't recall at the moment. What was it with me and girls and swimming pools? Would my good luck extend to rivers and lakes and creeks? Why was I wondering about stuff like that right now?

I began to lean toward her. Other thoughts were going through my head. How was my breath? Do Mormons kiss differently than other people? Is it wrong to kiss a girl when you don't even know her last name?

I was just inches away — even had my eyes closed — when she said, "Wait!"

I stopped. Extreme bummer. Maybe I'd misinterpreted the situation.

"My dad went to Provo to see my brother last weekend!" she said, and she sprang from the couch and hurried down the hallway again.

What the heck? What did that have to do with anything? I reluctantly rose from the couch and followed her. She was in her parents' bedroom again, kneeling, reaching under the bed. She dragged out a black suitcase and started going through the various pockets and compartments. Now I understood. A man with a back problem would take his pills with him when he traveled.

Michele began tossing things to the side — a pair of socks, a belt, a paperback novel. Her dad wasn't much of an unpacker. Then she held up a small leather pouch. His shaving kit, which looked a lot like Opa's.

She unzipped it and immediately said, "Yes!" She reached in and came out with another prescription bottle. Checked the label and said, "Score!"

This was the best of all possible developments, and I'm not lying when I say I was very happy about it, but as silly as it sounds, I was also still thinking about that moment on the couch. I still wanted to kiss her. And maybe I'd get the chance. Maybe, after we celebrated about her success, we'd pick up where we'd left off.

That's when I heard a sound. A deep, mechanical groaning from the other side of the house. I recognized it, of course. A garage door was going up.

Michele's eyes went wide. "My mom's home!"

I could describe my disappointment, and my sudden panic

at the thought of getting caught in the house by an angry mother, but I'll make a long story short: Michele shoved the prescription bottle into my hand and hustled me out the back door — yes, I was sneaking out another back door — with the quickest of goodbyes. No kiss. No swapping phone numbers. Not even a handshake.

13

If Mr. Gardner's name seems to be coming up a lot, that's because he was my favorite teacher. He made freshman English fun, and I can still remember one particular class discussion we had about irony. He said it can be one of the most powerful literary techniques a writer can use, and his favorite story involving irony was "The Gift of the Magi" by O. Henry.

What happens is, a young married couple doesn't have enough money to buy Christmas gifts. But the woman has this really long, beautiful hair, so she cuts it off and sells it to a wigmaker. Then she uses the money to buy her husband a chain for his pocket watch, which has been in his family for generations. Nice of her, huh? What she doesn't know is that he sold the watch to buy a cool set of combs for her hair. It's supposed to show the sacrifices they are willing to make for each other, but they both end up with gifts they have no use for, which is pretty darned ironic.

Here's something else ironic: It turned out that the lowlife scumbag slime ball who'd stolen our things had also done us a huge favor. Not on purpose, of course, and it didn't work out well for him at all, which made it even more ironic. Less than three hours after the jerk had taken our things, he'd already been arrested. How did I know this? While I was following Michele around as she searched her house, the arrest was making the national news.

When I got back to the motel, Opa was awake in bed, propped up by pillows, watching TV. It was still very cold in the room. Before I could even say anything, he held up a hand in a wait-a-minute gesture. For a second, I thought he had a grimace on his face, but then I realized it was an amused smirk, like he'd just heard a good joke. I closed the door behind me and sat on the edge of my bed, facing the TV. Rudi Villarreal was sharing a breaking story on CNN's Headline News.

I should stop right here and mention something. If adults want to find a way to get teenage boys interested in world events, hiring a news anchor who looks like Rudi Villarreal is a good start. Compared to some of those old dudes that used to be on *60 Minutes*, which my parents watch every Sunday, it's no contest. Regardless, I quickly forgot about Rudi Villarreal's appearance when I tuned in to the actual words coming out of her mouth.

"...a strange twist in the case of Henry and Charlie Dunbar, the grandfather and grandson who were first reported missing from Abilene, Texas, on Tuesday. Those of you following this story know that Henry Dunbar suffers from a terminal illness and is presumed to be traveling to Washington or Oregon to take advantage of those states' laws regarding physician-assisted suicide. Authorities are now saying that they were able to track a cell phone purchased by Henry Dunbar to Grand Canyon National Park, where it was used yesterday morning."

I began to put the pieces together. Opa and I had been smart enough to stop using his credit card, but it hadn't occurred to us that we shouldn't use the cell phones we'd bought with that card. It was so obvious now. Once the cops knew what we'd bought, it would be easy for them to figure out where and when the phone was used. So even though I'd learned a lot when I'd made that call to listen to Ranger David, the cops had learned a lot, too. Like our exact location. Those old ladies at the Grand Canyon were the least of our worries.

I returned my attention to the story. Now CNN was showing a clip of a familiar gray-haired man in a suit, with his name and title on the screen. It was our old friend Walter Hoggins, the chief of police in Abilene. He said, "We were able to track this particular phone up the interstate from Arizona into Utah, and the Salt Lake City police arrested an individual in possession of the phone this morning. His name is Steven Lee Dabbs and he appears to have no knowledge of the Dunbars or their whereabouts. Unfortunately, Mr. Dabbs has asked for an attorney and won't tell us how he came into possession of the phone. He'll be arraigned in the morning, and then we might be able to cut some sort of deal with him."

Now they switched back to Rudi Villarreal, who said, "Police Chief Hoggins later clarified that Dabbs has been arrested for drug possession in violation of a probated sentence on a previous conviction for burglary." She gave her viewers a very small but unmistakably playful smile. "As to the whereabouts of Henry Dunbar and his grandson Charlie, their current location is anybody's guess."

I looked at Opa and saw that he was still grinning. He said, "That's the third time they've run that report and I like it better each time. That'll teach him to steal from the Dunbars."

I thought it was great, that the thief got nailed, but I was also concerned about something. "Did you hear what the police chief said?"

"Which part?"

"He said they tracked the phone from Arizona to Utah."

"Yeah?"

"I only used the phone one time, at the Grand Canyon. If they were able to track it while we were traveling, that means you don't even have to use the phone for them to know where it is."

Opa nodded. "It probably only has to be turned on. I believe it bounces a signal off each tower as you pass by."

We both looked at his suitcase at the same time. His phone was in the suitcase.

"Relax," he said. "I haven't even taken it out of the package."

"You sure it has to be turned on?"

"Pretty sure. If it didn't, they'd be knocking on our door by now, wouldn't they?"

"Yeah, I guess so."

"See there, Bud? You were moping around because you left the car door unlocked. Turned out to be a blessing in disguise. Goes to show you never know how these things will work out."

Opa looked and sounded better than he had this morning. Maybe the sleep had helped him out, or maybe that pain pill from his shaving kit was still working. Or maybe the pain had gone away on its own. Yesterday, in the car, Opa had said there were highs and lows. Maybe the pain would be back in thirty minutes or an hour.

I remembered the prescription bottle in the pocket of my cargo shorts. I took them out and handed them to him. He looked at the label for about ten seconds, then he looked at me.

"Where did you get these?"

"Remember that girl I told you about?"

"The one by the pool."

"Yeah. She had them at her house. She took me over there. It's right down the street."

"Whose are they? Who is Donald Macon?"

"Her dad. He has a bad back. It's not the same medicine you take, but I bet it'll work."

He set the bottle on the nightstand and turned the volume

down on the TV. "But how did she know I needed painkillers?"

"When I went back outside, she called me over to the pool. I thought she was just being friendly, but she recognized me from the news. She was cool about it, though. She's not going to tell anyone. Anyway, we started talking, and I told her what was happening. That the trip was over because your medicine was gone."

"Whose idea was it to steal her dad's prescription?"

Steal? Was that really the right word, considering the circumstances? Heck, the man's own daughter had come up with the idea.

"Hers. We didn't steal it. She gave it to me."

"You didn't have a problem with that? The prescription wasn't hers to give."

Uh-oh. Here we go.

"Her dad can get a refill. You need this medicine a lot more than he does. Besides, it had been sitting in his suitcase since last weekend, so he doesn't even need it right now."

"That's rationalizing, Bud. You know what that word means?"

"I think so."

"You're coming up with excuses to justify bad behavior."

That didn't seem fair to me. "If taking the pills was wrong, why is it okay for us to be here, right now, when everyone is looking for us? What we're doing — this whole trip — why isn't that bad behavior?"

"Some people, maybe a lot of people, would say that it is. But I don't happen to be one of those people."

"Well, who's to say you aren't rationalizing?"

He considered my question for a moment, then said, "Each person has to make up his or her own mind about something like that. And those pills. Let's say you're a medical researcher and you come up with a cure for a disease. All it takes is one little pill and people are healed instantly. But you're also a little bit greedy, so you want a bunch of money for each pill, even though it doesn't cost much to produce. Poor people are dying, but you're not too worried about that, because you think you deserve to be paid. So here's the question: Would it be okay for someone to break into your lab, steal the pills, and hand them out to the sick people?"

It seemed like an easy question. "I think so, yeah. Because I'm being selfish while people are dying, so it's okay, right?"

"I can't answer that for you. You have to decide that for yourself."

"So there isn't a right answer?"

"Well, *I* think there's a right answer, and you obviously do, too. But lots of people would disagree with us, and they are equally sure they're right. They would say the researcher's ambition and desire to make some money were what drove him to develop the medicine in the first place. Without that profit motive, the medicine wouldn't even exist. Then nobody could be healed."

Well, crap. I hadn't thought of it that way.

"This isn't a new conundrum," Opa said. "People have been debating this sort of thing for centuries. But now think of this situation. You're one of the people who needs that pill. But your neighbor does too, and he can't afford one, so he takes yours. Is he wrong to do that?"

"Definitely," I said.

"Why?"

"Because I needed the pill as much as he did."

"What if you're eighty years old and he's only twenty, so he has a lot more to gain by taking the pill?"

I didn't know what to say about that.

"Not always easy, is it?" Opa asked.

"It's still my pill. By stealing my pill, he's taking my life."

"For the record, I agree with you. On the other hand, what you said earlier — that I need the medicine more than this girl's dad does — you can't be sure that's true."

"But you're — " I stopped. I was going to say, *But you're dying.* I didn't want to think about that right now, and I doubted Opa would think that was a good reason for taking Donald Macon's pills. "But all he has is a bad back," I said instead.

"And it could give him every bit as much pain as my condition. Maybe more."

I was tired of talking about it. Regardless of where I'd gotten the pills, they were the answer to our problem. They would allow us to finish the trip. Why couldn't he see that?

"So what're we gonna do?" I asked.

He handed the prescription bottle to me. "I appreciate what you did, Bud. I really do. But you need to take those back. Tell your friend I said thank you, but I can't take those. Even if I wanted to, it wouldn't be smart for me to take something that wasn't prescribed for me. It might even be dangerous."

"Fine. I understand. But then what? We're just going to give up?" He started to answer, but I kept talking. "Don't worry about me, okay? Don't worry about what I'll have to see or whether you think that's fair. Okay? How about you let *me* make that call? And as far as I'm concerned, I still want to take you to Seattle. So don't even factor that into your decision. As long as you still want a driver, I'm here, and I want to be here. I'll understand if you just don't feel good enough to continue, but if you quit because you're worried about me — "

His hand went up again. I guess I'd made my point, so I shut up. Finally, the air conditioner cut off, and it was suddenly very quiet in the room.

Opa said, "The truth is, I go back and forth on this. I worry that I made a tremendous mistake by bringing you on this trip. You're just a kid, Bud. A smart kid, yeah, and not a kid for much longer, but right now, you're still a kid. On the other hand — I don't know if I should even get into this, but I will

— I worry that your parents don't give you quite enough freedom to make up your own mind about some things. To think for yourself. I can't tell you how wrong I think that is."

He paused, but I didn't say anything. I was pretty sure I understood what he meant. And I happened to agree with him. At least about *one* of my parents.

When Opa continued, he'd switched gears. "I do feel quite a bit better than I did a few hours ago. I don't know if it will last, but I hope it does. So here's what we'll do. You go back to your friend and return those pills. Then, on your way back, see if you can find a drug store and get some good migraine medicine. Extra strength. Then we'll wait and see how I feel tomorrow morning."

Yes!

"So we'll stay here another night?" I hadn't expected that part, but I had no problem with it. You can probably guess where my mind was going.

"That's the plan."

"Are you hungry?" I sure was.

"At the moment, yeah. For some reason, I have a craving for fast food. French fries. I don't ever eat that junk."

"You want me to get some?"

"Yeah, why not. A greasy burger every once in awhile isn't a big deal. But before you go, there's something else I want to do. Something we should've done a few days ago."

"What?"

I noticed that the smirk was back on his face. He was up to something. He grabbed the pushbutton phone off the nightstand.

14

If we could've gone online, it would've been a lot easier to track down the number we needed. There was a phone book in the nightstand drawer, but it was for local numbers only, so it wasn't any help. So we had to do things the hard way. The long way. The way people did things before the Internet.

Opa started by dialing the number for Information. I was this close to laughing. I couldn't believe he was doing this. It made me nervous, like you feel when you make a prank phone call. I could only hear one side of the conversation.

Opa said, "I need the number for CNN, please...Yes, in Atlanta, Georgia." A few seconds later, he wrote the number on a notepad. "Thank you." He hung up and dialed the number. Waited. Then he had to push a button on the keypad. Then another button...and another button. He was navigating through a voice menu system. Then, finally, he said, "My name is Henry Dunbar. I'm trying to reach Rudi Villarreal. It's very important."

It took a solid fifteen minutes — during which time Opa had to repeat himself to about a dozen different people, most of whom didn't seem to believe a word he was saying — but he was finally put on the line with Rudi Villarreal's assistant, or her producer, or her producer's assistant, or something like that.

Then Opa totally and completely freaked me out by handing the phone to me.

"What're you doing?" I asked.

"Talk to her."

"About what?"

"Just talk to her. Quick, before she hangs up. You'll know what to say."

I held the phone to my year. "Uh, hello?"

"Who is this?" It sounded like a young woman.

"Charlie Dunbar."

"Right. We've gotten about three hundred calls from Charlie Dunbar in the past two days. What's your middle name?" She had a midwestern accent and not much patience.

"Philip."

"This home you broke into on Saturday — where is it?"

She was testing me to make sure I really was Charlie Dunbar, but she didn't have to be a bitch about it. "We didn't break in. The front door was open. It's on a street called LaSalle."

"Yeah, okay. What did your friend Matt take from the house?"

How would she know the answer to that question? Then I realized CNN had probably gained access to police reports. But the answer itself was so insignificant, it was doubtful any of the news networks would have mentioned it. So, for her purposes, it was a perfect question.

"A cordless drill," I said. Then I added, "Blue. Eighteen-volt model."

The next words out of her mouth could have come from a different person. That's how much her tone changed. Much nicer. "Charlie. Okay. My name is Eileen. Sorry I doubted you.

It's just that we've had all kinds of nutcases calling us."

"That's okay. I understand."

Eileen didn't even bother asking *why* I called, or maybe she didn't care, but she sure didn't waste any time with small talk. "You know what I'd love to do? I'd love to put you on the air right now. Live. Are you up for that?"

"Right now?"

"Well, right after the next break. Six minutes. Rudi is in the middle of her shift and I'm sure she'd have a bunch of questions for you."

"I don't think I want to do that. I don't want to go on the air."

"It's not a big deal, Charlie. No different than talking to me on the phone right now." She was trying to sound all reassuring and convincing.

"No, I'd rather not."

"Okay, well, can I ask you some questions and record it for the program?"

I thought about it. "That would be okay."

"Great. Give me just a few seconds. Hang on."

Eileen put me on hold and I heard some cheesy music. But it didn't take long. She was back in less than a minute, and she picked up right where she'd left off, firing away with her first question.

"Charlie, where are you right now?"

"Uh..."

"Just kidding. Can you tell us where you and your grandfather are headed?"

"I'd better not."

"But it's the northwest, right? Without getting specific."

I said, "No comment." I'd seen people say that on the news.

She laughed. "Well, you can't blame a girl for trying. So how are you doing? I mean, in general. Emotionally, physically."

"I'm doing fine. It's been a long trip, but it's important and I'm glad we're doing it."

I was pretty sure I could hear somebody else talking to her. Maybe several people, like she had a couple of co-workers in the room with her, suggesting questions.

She said, "How is your grandfather's health?"

"I'd rather not talk about that. I don't think that's anyone's business."

"Fair enough. It has to be difficult for a boy of your age to deal with all the responsibility that's been placed on your shoulders."

"I'm not sure what you mean."

"Charlie, you do understand why your grandfather is going on this trip, right?"

"Of course I do."

"Well, what I'm saying is, it must be hard to know that you're helping your grandfather make that kind of journey. A lot of kids wouldn't be comfortable with that. There are some people who think it's very irresponsible for your grandfather to have taken you along."

I was starting to get mad. "Look. My grandfather is sick. Everybody knows that. What he decides to do as far as doctors and treatment and all that — that's his business. Not yours, not mine, or anybody else's. But I know he needs me right now, and I love him, and that's why I'm here. If the tables were turned, he would do the exact same thing for me."

She didn't miss a beat. "What about your parents? They didn't give you permission to go on this trip. They're pretty upset."

I wasn't sure how to respond. Not that I didn't have plenty of thoughts running through my head. I most definitely did. What I wanted to say was, "My parents aren't upset because I went on a trip with my grandfather; they're upset because they think he shouldn't be going to see the doctor in Seattle. They can't imagine why he'd make a decision like that, so they haven't spent a single minute looking at things from his point of view. Instead of trying to understand why he's doing this, all they've done is try to come up with reasons why he's wrong. That doesn't seem fair to me at all. It's his life, and it's his decision. The rest of us should butt out."

Of course, I didn't say any of that. Maybe I'd give that speech later, directly to my parents, or maybe I wouldn't, but I couldn't say it now, to a national audience. Instead, what I said was, "No comment."

I was really, really hoping Michele would be at the pool again when I went outside. That would've made things a lot easier.

But she wasn't.

So how was I going to get the medicine back to her? I didn't think it would be smart to just walk right up to the door and knock. Not with her mother there. Talking to a librarian, or smiling at a couple of old ladies at the Grand Canyon — that was as far as I was willing to push my luck. After all, Michele's mom, if she was like most moms, would be curious about this new boy hanging around her daughter. She'd ask me questions and really check me out, and that meant she might recognize me. My experience with Michele had taught me that I was still recognizable, even with my buzz haircut.

So how was I going to do it?

Knock on her bedroom window? Not a chance. I could be mistaken as a peeping Tom or a burglar.

I couldn't call or text her, because I didn't know her number, and even if I did, I couldn't use my cell phone. So even if I knew her number, I'd have to use a pay phone, if I could find one.

But wait. Now I had a different idea. I couldn't call her, no, but I could call someone else. Someone who could get on Facebook, find Michele's page, and contact her for me.

Matt.

"Dude, you are sick! I've been going crazy! Why haven't you called me? They're playing you on CNN right now! Everybody's talking about it! Where are you?"

"If I tell you, you can't tell anyone."

"I won't."

I'd managed to find a pay phone in a convenience store parking lot near the interstate. "I'm serious, Matt. You hear me? You can't tell a single person." I really didn't want to tell him where we were, but he'd figure it out anyway when I asked him to get on Facebook to find Michele Macon. Her hometown would be listed.

"I promise," he said.

"Salt Lake City."

"You're in Nevada?"

"Utah, you moron."

"I meant Utah. Are you going to Seattle, like everybody's saying?"

I hated to lie to him, but he wasn't the best at keeping secrets. I was willing to tell him where we were right now, because we'd be leaving in the morning, but telling him where we were going — that was something else entirely. "I don't know yet. We might go to Portland instead, or maybe even Spokane. Opa hasn't decided. He even mentioned Eugene. Says that's a really nice area."

Matt changed the subject abruptly and launched into a long-winded story of everything that had happened to him since I'd left. This was when I learned about his run-in with Cathy Abbott's wrestler boyfriend, all the details about how he'd been arrested and spent the night in jail, and why he'd finally broken down the next morning and told the cops I'd been with him when he took the drill. "That way, the guy who owned the drill wouldn't press charges. It seemed like we'd both get in less trouble that way," Matt said, sounding apologetic.

"Don't worry about it."

"Besides, with everything that's going on, I don't think I'm gonna get in much trouble now. You sorta provided a big distraction, taking off with your grandpa. I think my parents are secretly thrilled that all I did was take a drill."

I didn't know whether to feel good or bad about that. It was starting to occur to me that each of my friends and their family members would have an opinion about what Opa and I were doing. Some of them would support us, but some of them — maybe a lot of them — would feel the same way as my parents about this situation. I didn't like thinking about that, so I said, "Where are you right now?"

"In my room. I'm grounded 'for the foreseeable future,' is what my dad said."

"Did they take away your computer?"

"No, thank God. I'd be going crazy. But my mom's always coming in and poking around, to see what I'm doing. So I've got it set for private browsing. She has no clue what that is."

"I need you to get on Facebook."

He laughed. "I'm not supposed to."

"But you will, right?"

"Of course, because my mom's not here right now. Why am I getting on Facebook?"

I told him I needed him to find Michele Macon in Salt Lake City.

"Who is she?"

"Just a girl."

I could hear him typing away. Then he said, "Whoa. A *hot*

girl."

"What does she look like?"

"Wait, I thought you knew her."

"I do, but I want to make absolutely sure it's the same one."

"Okay, well, she's about our age, with blond hair. And she's hot."

"You already said that." I waited as he looked at her profile. He didn't say anything for awhile, so I said, "Does she have a brother named Tim?"

"Hold on."

I held on.

"Yeah, she does."

"Okay, that's her. I need you to send her a message."

"Oh, this is funny. I just noticed that her status says, 'Met someone famous today. Can't tell you who. But he's cute.' Is she talking about you?"

15

I hung around the parking lot and started scoping out the vehicles stopping at the convenience store. Most of the vehicles were cars, not trucks, and a lot of the drivers looked like locals who were just stopping to buy cigarettes or fill up with gas. The trucks I did see all had Utah license plates.

Then, finally, an old Ford F-150 with Wyoming plates pulled in and parked in front of the store. I watched the driver hop out and go inside. I wished I could follow him inside and strike up a casual conversation. Maybe find out where he was going. Was he on his way back to Wyoming? But, again, I couldn't take that chance. I needed to keep my interaction with people at a bare minimum. Besides, the convenience store was right on the interstate, so the odds were pretty good that this man was traveling.

I'd already taken Opa's cell phone out of the packaging earlier, so now I pulled the phone out of my pocket and turned it on as I approached the man's truck. When I got within ten feet, I could see that the bed of the truck had all sorts of junk in it. Some old tires and pieces of scrap lumber. Perfect.

I walked along the side of the truck and, in a very quick

move, without slowing down, I stuck the phone inside one of the old tires. I was pretty slick about it. Nobody saw me. Then I walked around the front of the truck and went into the store.

There was a middle-aged lady behind the counter, but she was busy with a customer, so she didn't look my way. I found the aisle with a small selection of medicine and picked out some extra-strength migraine tablets. A large bottle. The price was nearly eight dollars. Then I grabbed a candy bar.

When I went to pay, the guy from Wyoming was at the counter, buying a six-pack of Mountain Dew and a king-sized bag of almonds. After he left, I placed my items on the counter.

"Ooh boy, I hope you ain't got a bad one," the cashier lady said as she rang the items up. She had a voice like a shovel being dragged on pavement.

"Huh?" I was busy watching the guy from Wyoming get into his F-150.

She shook the bottle. "Migraine. I get 'em myself. Worse than giving birth. Eeyow." She let out a really big, shrieky laugh, and I saw that several of her teeth were missing. And now, up close, I could see that her face was pretty wrinkly. She was older than I first thought, or she'd spent too much time in the sun.

"They're for my mother," I said. I looked out the window again. The F-150 was pulling onto the access road.

The cashier said, "Aw, you're a sweet kid, takin' care of your momma," and as she looked at me, her eyebrows furrowed. "You come in here before?"

"Yes, ma'am. I live a few blocks away."

She was nodding. "Yeah, I thought you looked familiar. I reco'nize most of my customers."

Another glance out the window. The F-150 was pulling up the ramp, onto the interstate. Exactly what I had hoped to see. I wondered how far he would make it before the cops tracked him down.

"Watcha wanna do," the lady said, "is give your momma some peace and quiet. Maybe slip her a glass of whiskey, then stay outta her hair for a few hours. She'll be good as new." She winked at me and let out another shriek.

I stopped at a Radio Shack in a strip center and bought another prepaid cell phone — paying with cash. Then I stopped at a McDonald's and got four Big Macs and four large fries to go. I hoped Opa was still hungry. I'd noticed he hadn't eaten as much in the past day or so. I guess his stomach wasn't feeling well, which was why he'd thrown up this morning.

When I got back to the motel — by now it was almost two in the afternoon — he was sitting up in bed, reading a book. CNN was still on the TV. "You're the top story. They've been playing your interview every ten or fifteen minutes," he said. "Of course, they'll get tired of that, just like everything else. The attention span of the American public is a pitiful thing. How'd it go?"

I handed him the migraine pills.

"Perfect. Thank you."

I handed him the bulging bag from McDonald's.

"I can't tell you how good that smells," he said, shaking his head like it was a strange occurrence. Funny, because fast food always smells good to me, even after I'm stuffed.

Opa handed me a Big Mac. As he unwrapped one for himself, he said, "What about the girl?"

"Michele."

"Right. Did you get that sorted out?"

"I'm meeting her tonight."

He raised one eyebrow. "Tonight, huh?"

***

I sat on a bench near the sand volleyball pit and waited. This place was called Jordan Park, and it was about a ten-minute walk from the motel, sort of in the direction of Michele's house, but a little to the south.

There weren't many people around. Nobody was playing volleyball. I'd passed a baseball field, but nobody was playing there, either. Of course, it was a Thursday evening. Things were probably a little livelier around here on the weekend. I'd seen one guy walking two enormous Great Danes. Long shadows were creeping across the ground, but there was still at least an hour of light left.

"Hey."

I turned around. Michele was coming up behind me, wearing a white tank top, a denim skirt, and sandals. She looked great. Her hair was hanging loose around her tan, freckled shoulders.

"Hey," I said back.

She sat beside me. "My mom totally busted me. She knew a boy was in the house." Then, before I could say anything, she said, "Just kidding. So what's the deal? Your grandpa doesn't want the pills?"

She wasn't being catty about it, just being curious, because I hadn't told her much through Matt. He'd messaged her, and she had immediately messaged back, and I told Matt what to say, and here we were.

I said, "Well, Opa wanted me to tell you he said thanks, but he didn't think he should take them."

"Why not?"

"Mostly because they aren't his. He's really...I don't know how to explain it. He's very principled. He just always does what he thinks is right. More than any other person I know."

"That's pretty cool."

"I think so. Sometimes it's a pain."

"I was doing what I thought was right, too, you know. When I gave you the pills."

"Yeah, I know. He knows that, too. It meant a lot to him that you were willing to do that. To me, too. It meant a lot to me."

I took the prescription bottle out of my pocket and handed it to her. She stuck it in the small purse she was carrying.

Now what?

"This is a pretty neat park," I said.

"Yeah, it's okay. There are a couple of tennis courts over there." She pointed vaguely past a grove of trees.

"Do you play?" I asked.

"District champion."

"Really?"

"You bet. Two years in a row. How do you think I got these great legs?"

I'm pretty sure she was just trying to make me turn red. Which I did.

"I'm glad I got to see you again," I said, and somehow, it didn't sound as dorky as it might have.

She cocked her head to one side and looked at me. "You wanna see the peace gardens?"

"The what?"

On one side of the park, along the banks of the Jordan River, was a place called the International Peace Gardens. I'll do my best to describe it. It was basically separate garden areas — with statues and sculptures, arbors and crushed gravel walkways — representing the cultures of various countries. I thought it would be corny, but it was actually pretty cool. Everything was lush and healthy and colorful, with more kinds of flowers than I can name or remember.

The Chinese garden had a pair of concrete lions acting as sentries on either side of a pagoda. The Swiss garden centered around a towering rock monument shaped like the Matterhorn. The Dutch garden featured a windmill and a gigantic wooden shoe filled with tulips.

"They have a lot of weddings in the gardens," Michele said.

We were sitting on a bench in the Indian garden, which featured a large statue of Buddha. We hadn't seen anybody else in at least ten minutes. The sun was below the tree line.

"Yeah, I can see why." It was very quiet here. Maybe the plants somehow sucked up the noise of the surrounding city.

"People get married in the garden that represents where their ancestors came from. Like people with German ancestors get married in the German garden."

"Makes sense. But what if the man is from Sweden and the woman is from Canada?"

"Maybe they have the wedding in one garden and the reception in the other."

I noticed that her thigh was touching my thigh, and I didn't think it was an accident. She was right earlier when she said she had great legs.

"If I were to get married here," Michele said, "it would be in the Scottish garden."

"You're Scottish?"

"On my mom's side. We don't know about my dad's side because he was adopted."

She was just making small talk. I knew that. She was making small talk until I worked up the nerve to kiss her. Why was it so hard, even when I was fairly certain she wanted me to do it?

"We're mostly English," I said. "I had one great-grandmother who was German, but most of my ancestors were English."

"Top of the morning to you," she said, in a really poor accent.

"That sounds more like Irish."

"It does? How do you tell the difference?"

"Well, one's English and one's Irish."

She bumped me with her elbow. "Smartass. Let's hear you do it."

I made a big show of preparing myself, like an actor getting ready to go on stage. Then I did my best Austin Powers imitation. "Allow myself to introduce...myself. My name is Richie Cunningham, and this is my wife, Oprah."

It worked. Michele started to laugh. Hard. So, of course, I kept going.

"This is me in a nutshell: 'Help, I'm in a nutshell! How did I get into this bloody great big nutshell? What kind of shell has a nut like this?'"

It feels good to make a pretty girl crack up like that. Finally, when she stopped, she said, "So, not to be a downer, but when are you leaving?"

"Tomorrow morning."

We both sat quietly for a minute.

"I worry about you and your grandpa in that car."

"It runs great. We'll be fine."

"No, what I mean is, if anything's going to get you caught, it's the car. The police will be looking for that car, and they seem to have a pretty good idea where you're going."

"There's not much we can do about that. There's no way we can get another car."

Buddha seemed to be staring at me. I wondered what he was thinking.

"Will you stay in touch?" Michele asked.

"If I'm not in prison."

She laughed again. I was on a roll. "You'd look cute in those striped clothes they make prisoners wear."

"You think?"

"Yeah, I do think."

"I don't think they use stripes anymore. I'm pretty sure they make them wear orange, which would totally clash with my complexion."

She took my chin in her hand and turned my head from side to side, appearing to examine the tone of my skin. "I'd say you're a spring. You need to wear warm colors."

Our faces were about a foot apart.

"Warm colors?" I said. "What does that mean?"

"Peaches. Yellows. Like that."

And that's when I finally worked up the guts. Turns out Mormons kiss just like everybody else.

16

"This is way cool," I said.

"I told you it would be."

"I had no idea."

It was nine-thirty on Friday morning, and Opa and I were more than one hundred miles west of Salt Lake City, driving through the Bonneville Salt Flats. We'd gotten up early, but before we'd left, we were faced with a question: Which way to go?

At this point, there were only so many routes to choose from, unless we got completely off the interstates in favor of smaller roads. As usual, it was a balance. We didn't want to waste much time, but we didn't want to get caught, either.

Interstate 15 up to I-84 was the shortest, most obvious route, but that was the problem with it: It was the most obvious route. We didn't want to be obvious. Sticking on I-15 all the way into Montana, then taking a left on I-90 — that would've been my second choice.

But Opa had suggested going west on I-80 out of Salt Lake City so we could see the salt flats. In fact, he was fairly insistent on it.

"Then what?" I'd asked, looking at the map. "Take I-80 all the way over to Sacramento? That's gotta be four or five hundred miles out of the way."

"No, we'll take one of these state highways," he said, pointing. "I think 95 looks good."

"Which will take us back to I-84, and I thought we agreed to avoid that."

"Then we could just stay on 95 into Idaho, past Clearwater National Forest. We can work our way over to Spokane, then take 2 over to Seattle, or pretty close."

"That doesn't look like much of a highway," I said.

"Where's your sense of adventure?"

He seemed to be feeling pretty well this morning, all things considered, but it had become obvious that that could change in a matter of hours, if not minutes. That sort of took the adventure out of me. I just wanted to get him to Seattle as soon as possible. I'd seen two highway patrol vehicles this morning, and I'd held my breath each time, but they'd zipped passed us in the opposite direction without taking notice. How long would our luck hold out? Probably not long if we stayed on the interstates. Ultimately, we'd agreed that we'd take state highways and we'd occasionally jump onto an interstate as necessary. And we'd start that plan just as soon as we'd passed through the salt flats.

"Is it really just salt?" I asked. As we cruised along the interstate, there was an immense white plain stretching for miles on either side of the car. I'd never seen anything like it.

"Yep, just like regular old table salt. You could scrape up a handful and throw it on your supper."

"Why is it all here?"

"All of this used to be underwater. The ocean is gone, but the salt was left behind."

"But why? I mean, there are a lot of places that were once underwater, right? So why aren't there salt flats in all those places?"

"Good question. That'll give you something to look up later."

"You mean you don't know?"

"Nope. I'm sure there's a logical reason. Ask your science teacher and see how happy it makes him that you care about something like that."

"Her. There's only one science teacher for sophomores — Mrs. Townsend."

"Okay, ask her."

I had to smile. "I can't believe I finally asked a question you couldn't answer."

"Don't you worry, there are a lot of questions I can't answer."

"Name another."

There was only a slight pause before he said, "Okay, how did we get here?"

"Well, first we went west on I-20 out of Lubbock...."

He knew I was kidding around. He said, "The thing is, when we don't know the answer to a question like that, it's tempting to fill in the blank with...*something*. Maybe we'll know the answer someday, and maybe we won't, but there's no shame in saying, 'I don't know.' No sense in making something up."

There was very little traffic on the interstate, so I was able to go slow and just enjoy the scenery. I found myself gazing at the mountain peaks on the horizon beyond the salt flats. It was like some strange landscape on another planet. Sort of like that scene in *Star Wars* where Luke is riding that floating vehicle across the plains. I almost expected to look up and see an extra moon in the sky. Okay, not really, I'm just making a point.

I was thinking about the way the Grand Canyon was formed. "How come there aren't big ruts through the salt from erosion?"

"That, I can answer. Every winter, the flats are flooded by a thin layer of water, and that sort of smoothes everything out. When the water evaporates, it's like a brand new surface. It's perfect for racing. Ever hear of the Blue Flame?"

"I think so. It was a rocket car or something."

"Yep, and it set the land speed record of more than six hundred miles per hour. That was in 1970. Then, in the nineties, some guy broke the sound barrier over in Nevada."

"How fast?"

"I can't recall exactly. Seven sixty something."

I couldn't even imagine that. "Man, if we could go that fast, we'd be in Seattle by now."

"And just think of everything we would've missed," Opa said.

He fell asleep for several hours after that, so it was up to me to navigate. When I reached Wells, Nevada, I took 93 up through Twin Falls, Idaho, then I got on I-84. The towns and cities zipped past. Jerome, Wendell, Bliss, Mountain Home. This part of Idaho reminded me of parts of Texas. Not the pretty parts.

Opa woke a little later, stretched and said, "Where are we?"

"Coming up on Boise."

He nodded and picked up the map.

"How are you feeling?" I asked.

He raised his head and truly thought about it. "Pretty darn good, actually. I could use a rest stop soon, and something to eat. After that, I suggest we go west on 20 and eventually work our way over to I-5. They won't be expecting us to come up from that direction."

And that's what we did. Just thirty minutes after Boise, we crossed over into Oregon, and even though neither of us said anything about it, I considered it a victory of sorts. Oregon was one of the two states that allowed assisted suicide. We'd made it that far. Now, just a little farther. It all seemed within our grasp. By the time we found another mom-and-pop motel in the town of Bend at nine that evening — meaning we were now just six or seven hours from Seattle — I thought we were home free.

Of course, I was way wrong.

17

The state police cruiser appeared behind us at 10:14 the next morning, two hours after we'd left Bend, as we were making our way through the Mt. Hood National Forest on State Highway 26.

One minute my rearview mirror was empty, and the next I could see a vehicle zooming up on me at tremendous speed. At first I thought it might be a park ranger. But, nope, it was a trooper, in a dark-brown Crown Victoria, with a heavy-duty grille guard and a low-profile light bar on the roof. I was really surprised to see a trooper on that stretch of road meandering through the evergreens, so far from the major highways. He came up on us so fast, as if he were in a hurry to get somewhere, that I was hoping he'd go around our little Honda.

He didn't.

"Opa?"

He'd had his eyes shut for several miles, but I could tell by his breathing that he wasn't asleep. "Yeah?"

"There's a state trooper behind us."

He opened his eyes but he didn't sit up. "For how long?"

"He just appeared out of nowhere. Maybe he was hiding

somewhere along the road."

"Were you speeding?"

"No."

"What's he doing?"

"Just following us. Pretty close, too. Like, right on my bumper."

"But no lights on?"

"Nope."

We drove another few hundred yards.

Opa said, "It's kind of tough for him to pass right here. Let's wait and see if he passes when he gets a chance."

A half-mile later, there was a stretch where the trooper could have gone around us easily. No traffic at all. He stayed where he was.

Opa eased up a little straighter and glanced casually into the passenger-side mirror.

"What should we do?" I asked.

"Well, there's not a lot we can do."

"Should I pull over and see if he passes then? If he wants us, why isn't he turning on his siren?"

"I don't know."

All I could think of was the Texas license plate on the rear of the car. Might as well be a neon sign. I could clearly see the trooper in the mirror. "It looks like he's talking to somebody. He has a microphone in his hand, I think." My voice sounded higher than it normally does. I was nervous.

"Just settle down, Bud. It's going to be okay."

Several miles went by and the trooper remained behind us. Not doing anything, just following. Close. No lights, no siren.

The highway widened to four lanes as we approached a small community called Government Camp. The trooper did not pass. On the other side of town, the road went back to two lanes, and that's when the trooper finally switched on his lights. My mirror was filled with flashing red and blue. Opa let out a little groan. Oddly, I was calmer now than I was before. I'd been expecting this. I kept driving.

Opa was still watching the trooper in the passenger mirror. "Bud?"

"Yeah?"

"Are you going to pull over?"

I didn't answer right away.

"Bud?"

"I don't know. Do you think I ought to?"

He chuckled, which I wasn't expecting. "What's the alternative?"

"Just keep driving. Not fast. Just like we're driving now."

"Just keep driving?"

"Yeah."

He was giving it some thought. Finally, he said, "That might not be a bad idea."

It wasn't like we were racing around curves. There was no danger to anyone. I wasn't going to try to outrun the police. That would've been crazy. But I wasn't ready to give up. We were so close. We were about an hour from Portland, and from there it was a straight shot up Interstate 5 to Seattle.

"Pull over!"

Boy, I jumped. The trooper was using the loudspeaker mounted behind his front grille, and *loud*speaker was absolutely the right name for it. It was like he was sitting in the backseat of our car with a bullhorn.

"This is the Oregon State Police! Pull over to the side of the road!"

I didn't. I wasn't going to. "Do you think he knows who we are?" I asked Opa.

"Without a doubt."

"So he knows we aren't dangerous."

"Well, he should."

We came upon a beat-up old Chevy truck moseying down

the highway, but the driver pulled over to the shoulder and let us pass when he saw the trooper's lights behind us.

"Will he try to stop us?" I asked.

"He's already trying."

"No, I mean like run us off the road or something."

"I can't imagine. I think he's going to be as careful with us as they've ever been with anybody."

"Why?"

"We're the biggest story in the news right now. They have to be real careful how they handle this. Whatever they do, it will be all over CNN in an hour."

CNN. Of course. Why hadn't that occurred to me?

"Opa, I bought another cell phone in Salt Lake City. It's in the glove compartment. My wallet's in there too, and in my wallet is that producer's phone number."

She'd given me her cell number at the end of our interview the day before. She told me to call her anytime, day or night. I glanced over for a second and saw that Opa was grinning at me. He knew exactly what I was thinking. He grabbed the cell phone, opened my wallet, then dialed the number. It seemed to take an awfully long time for the call to go through.

Then, finally, Opa said, "Eileen, this is Henry Dunbar... Yes...Uh huh...No, he's driving. Listen, an Oregon state trooper is following us right now and...About an hour outside Portland... Oregon...No, we're heading that way...On State Highway 26 right now...Yes, I'm sure they do, because of our license plate... No, we haven't, and we don't intend to. We plan to keep driving all the way to Seattle. I'm just letting you know, because, well, it's news, and it wouldn't bother me one bit if you decided to mention this on the air...No, they haven't, and I'm — "

"Pull your car to the shoulder!"

Opa continued. "Yeah, you could hear him, huh?...No, we're not running, we're just driving along, nice and slow.

Forty miles an hour. But the bottom line is that we haven't done anything wrong, and as far as I know, there isn't a warrant for my arrest, so we have no plans to stop. We want to finish what we started. We see no reason why they shouldn't just leave us alone...That's nice of you to ask. I feel very good right now. But mostly I'm proud of Charlie and I wouldn't change a thing about what we've done in the past four days....Okay... Yes, that's fine with me. Thank you very much."

He closed the phone.

"What'd she say?"

"That this will run as a breaking story within a few minutes."

Which was exactly what we were hoping. We wanted the eyes of the world to be focused on the Oregon state trooper behind us. Quickly.

Now we were passing through a tiny town called Rhododendron, which even had a Dairy Queen. I guess those are everywhere. A couple of customers standing outside turned and stared as we passed by. The road had opened up to four lanes again, but the trooper stayed right where he was.

Opa opened the phone again and punched in three numbers. It was easy to deduce that those three numbers were 911.

Three seconds later, he said, "My name is Henry Dunbar. My grandson and I...No, just listen. My grandson and I are driving through Mt. Hood National Forest with a trooper behind us. I suggest that you tune in to CNN before that trooper takes any further action."

He snapped the phone shut with a laugh. "Whoever that guy was, he wasn't very happy."

We left Rhododendron and the road went back to two lanes. Nothing happened for several miles. We just kept driving, and the trooper kept following, lights flashing, and he would occasionally tell us to pull over. When we'd come up behind other vehicles, the drivers would pull to the shoulder after a few minutes, when they saw what was going on behind them. We passed through a community called Zigzag, and another one called Mt. Hood Village, where the road went to four lanes and stayed that way, and then I saw the worst thing possible.

Another state trooper was waiting on the right side of the highway.

Before we reached him, he pulled onto the pavement in front of us and accelerated up to speed. This was not good. Now they had us boxed in. For the moment, the trooper in the lead was maintaining a steady forty miles per hour. But how long before he began to slow down, forcing us to either stop or attempt to go around him?

After ten or fifteen more minutes like this, the trees began to thin and I knew we were about to emerge on the west side of the forest. Portland wouldn't be long after that. The trooper behind us was yakking into his microphone; I could see him back there. Then he got on his loudspeaker one more time and told us to pull over. We didn't, of course, and that's when the troopers decided to make their move. Nothing dramatic. The trooper in front simply began to go slower and slower. He wasn't hitting the brakes, but he wasn't giving it any gas, either.

"Should I go around him?" I asked Opa. We were going thirty miles per hour.

"No, Bud. That's taking it too far."

He was right. Refusing to stop was one thing, but attempting to evade the troopers was something else entirely.

Now we were going twenty-five.

The cell phone rang. Opa still had it in his hand. "Hello?"

It had to be Eileen. Opa was listening intently.

We were going twenty miles per hour. Our Honda was sandwiched between the two troopers' cars.

"How soon?" Opa asked.

The trooper behind us couldn't have been more than ten feet from our bumper.

Opa leaned forward and looked toward the sky. "Not yet."

The troopers weren't attempting to guide me off the side of the road; we were simply going slower and slower in the far right-hand lane.

"There are two of them now," Opa said, "and they are bringing us to a stop."

Ten miles per hour. Just rolling.

"That's a good idea," Opa said. "I'll do that."

Five miles per hour.

Four.

Three.

And the trooper in front — now just a few feet from our grille — hit the brakes. So did I. All three vehicles came to a stop. Very slowly, the trooper in front backed his cruiser up until his bumper kissed ours. The trooper behind did the same thing. Now the Honda was locked in tight. After more than twenty-three hundred miles, our long journey from Abilene had come to an end.

Opa placed the phone, still open, on the dashboard.

"What was she saying?" I asked.

"Hold on." He was still looking skyward.

I heard it before I saw it, probably because of all the tall trees in the area.

Thump-thump-thump-thump...

And suddenly it appeared. A news helicopter. Hovering so low in front of us that I could see the face of the cameraman in the passenger's seat. I was so distracted by it, I didn't see the trooper at my door until he rapped on the window. He wore a light-blue shirt and a dark-blue tie, plus a wide, flat-brimmed hat that looked sort of military, like the ones the Canadian Mounties wear. His leather belt sagged under the weight of the big gun on his right hip.

162   **Ben Rehder**

"What should I do?" I asked Opa.

"Lower your window a couple of inches."

So I did.

The trooper, who actually looked like a nice enough guy, about my dad's age, said, "Please turn off your engine."

I did.

"Are both of you doing okay?" he asked.

"We are," Opa answered.

"Do either of you need medical attention?"

"No, we don't."

"May I see some identification, please?" This was directed at me.

"I, uh — "

"He doesn't have an ID yet," Opa said.

The trooper didn't look surprised. "What's your full name?"

I said, "Charles Philip Dunbar."

Now he looked at Opa. "May I see your identification, sir?"

Opa looked like he was about to say something — probably going to refuse the trooper's request — but then he changed his mind. He opened his wallet, removed his driver's license, and passed it to me. I slipped it to the trooper through the opening at the top of the window. He studied it briefly, then said, "Okay, I'm going to ask both of you to step out of the vehicle."

Opa said, "No disrespect, Officer, but we're going to stay where we are. We'd like to continue on our way."

The helicopter was still buzzing around up there, trying to get the best possible angle to record the scene. Now it was hovering over the trooper's left shoulder. I couldn't help it. I smiled and waved.

The trooper — his last name was Reeves, according to the little nametag on his uniform — said, "Sir, if you'll both exit the vehicle, we'll get this sorted out." Reeves didn't sound angry or impatient — just calm and polite, really. I noticed that his eyes were wandering over the interior of the car, including the backseat. I'm sure the troopers are trained to do that, so they'll know what they are dealing with.

"Thanks, but we'll stay in the car," Opa said.

The trooper didn't say anything for a few seconds, then he nodded and stepped away from the Honda. But he didn't go back to his cruiser. Instead, he walked just out of earshot and spoke into the microphone that was attached to his shirt, just below his left shoulder. I could see in the outside mirror that the other trooper was standing near the bumper of our car. Just standing there, watching.

There was nothing for us to do but wait, so we did. The helicopter seemed louder than before, so I looked up and saw that there were now two of them. I was amazed that they had gotten here so fast.

Opa said, "Here comes another one."

But he wasn't talking about helicopters, he was talking about troopers. Another cruiser was approaching from the west, and it pulled to the opposite shoulder and parked. The trooper, a tall, slender, dark-haired woman, got out and joined the trooper standing behind the Honda. I could see them talking back there.

This was getting silly. All of this attention and manpower for us. It was a waste. After about ten minutes, Reeves returned to the window.

"Looks like we could be here awhile," he said. "Either of you need something to drink?"

"No, we're fine, but thank you," Opa said. "What do you mean we could be here awhile? What's going on?"

"Sir, this is an unusual situation. I'm waiting to hear back from my superiors."

"What exactly are we waiting on?"

"I believe my boss is speaking to the state attorney general."

"About what?"

"I can't get any more specific than that."

"You can't just hold us here like this," Opa said.

"I'm afraid I can. I would appreciate your patience. Hang tight, please."

He left again, but he wasn't gone as long this time. When he came back, his eyes went to the cell phone resting on the dashboard. "Sir, I'm going to ask you to close that cell phone."

I hadn't picked up on it before, but now I realized that Eileen, the producer, was still on the other end, and that probably meant our conversation was being broadcast live on CNN. Somebody had informed Trooper Reeves of that fact.

Opa said, "I prefer to leave it open."

Reeves didn't take it personally. He nodded again — man, he had the perfect poker face! — and then he left us alone for the third time. This episode lasted about twenty minutes, during which time another trooper arrived, and, believe it or not, a third helicopter appeared on the horizon. It was like the cruisers and the helicopters were in a competition to outnumber each other. I realized that I hadn't seen another car — a civilian vehicle — in quite some time, and I wondered if there were yet more troopers stopping traffic a mile or two away in each direction.

Reeves finally came back. "Won't be long now," he said, as if we were all working together on some big plan to get this mess cleared up. He really did seem like a decent guy. He remained near the window.

"Where were you?" I asked.

"Pardon?"

"I never saw you until you were coming up behind us."

"Oh, I was working traffic detail — running radar — on the other side of Government Camp. When I saw a green

Honda Civic go past with Texas plates..." He didn't need to finish.

"It must be a pretty good hiding spot," I said.

"Yeah, it's tucked back in the trees. I've been using it for a long time."

There was a short pause.

"How long have you been a trooper?" Opa asked.

"Nineteen years."

We were obviously just making small talk to fill the time, but I didn't know what else to say or ask. That didn't matter, though, because right then the portable radio on Reeves's belt squawked. I didn't understand the garbled voice that came out, but Reeves seemed to have no trouble with it at all. He held up a finger toward us in a "give me a minute" gesture and stepped away from the Honda yet again. It had been nearly an hour since Reeves first pulled us over.

"What do you think's going on, Opa?"

He took the cell phone off the dashboard and covered the mouthpiece with his hand. "I have no idea."

"If they were gonna arrest us or something, you'd think they'd have done it already."

"I agree. But I don't think — "

He stopped talking, because Reeves was coming back. The trooper leaned in close to the window again. I never would have guessed what he was about to say.

"Okay, gentlemen, I appreciate your patience. Here's how we'd like to proceed. We will continue on Highway 26 into Portland until we hit Interstate 205. We will stay on 205 until it crosses the river, at which point Washington state troopers will take over and my troopers will — "

Opa couldn't help but interrupt. "Hold on a sec."

"Yes, sir?"

"What are you talking about?"

"The route we're going to take."

Now Opa snapped the cell phone shut. Goodbye, Eileen. Then he looked at Reeves and said, "Are you telling me that we're going to get a police escort into Seattle?"

Reeves pushed his hat back further on his head and smiled for the first time. "Sir, that's exactly what I'm saying."

The rest of our trip was like something out of a movie. Not some little independent movie, but a big, flashy summer blockbuster. Someday, when I tell my kids about it — and you can bet I will — they'll think I'm exaggerating or just flat-out making it up. Luckily, it's all on YouTube.

We started out with one trooper leading the way and two trailing behind us. And the helicopters followed, of course. Three of them. Later it was four, and then five, or maybe it was six. It was hard to keep track.

Opa turned the radio on — to the AM band, because those stations were more likely to carry news — and we were amazed at what we heard. We were the subject of conversation on every single station on the dial, except for one that was playing a Toby Keith song.

Other drivers began to pull up next to us in the left-hand lane so they could wave and give us the thumbs-up sign. Some took photos. Some of them lingered too long, and the troopers decided to put a stop to it. The two cruisers behind us started riding side by side, preventing any traffic from passing us. Opa called it a "rolling roadblock." He said the troopers back home used to do that before the big football game between Texas and Oklahoma in the Cotton Bowl. Troopers would ride side by side on Interstate 35 all the way from Austin to Dallas to prevent fans from speeding.

As we rolled through small towns like Woodland, Castle Rock, Napavine, and Fords Prairie, city police cars were parked in the middle of each lighted intersection, holding up traffic so our procession wouldn't have to stop. It was like we were part of a parade.

By the time we reached the outskirts of Tacoma, south of Seattle, we began to see an occasional car pulled to the side of the highway, with the driver and maybe a passenger or two waiting for us to pass by so they could cheer us on. Some of them held up homemade signs with words of support and encouragement.

GO CHARLIE AND HENRY!

WELCOME TO WASHINGTON!

IT'S HENRY'S CHOICE

As we got closer to the Seattle city limits, there were more and more people, more signs, news vans with cameramen standing on top for a better view, helicopters circling like mosquitoes, and police officers parked every quarter-mile or so to keep everything under control.

Opa and I hadn't spoken in several miles; we were too busy absorbing everything we were seeing. It was nothing short of a spectacle. Now Opa said, "This is...this..."

The cell phone rang. I had forgotten that Reeves had asked for the number. Opa answered, and I could tell from the conversation that the caller — someone from the Washington state police — needed to know where exactly we wanted to go in Seattle. Opa pulled a piece of paper from his wallet and gave the caller an address.

The doctor's office.

The police stopped traffic on each end of the block. We passed between two cruisers on the south end and our situation changed immediately. Suddenly, we were all alone. It was sort of freaky because it happened so quickly. Now it was just me and Opa and an empty street. No cops, no well-wishers, not even any news helicopters circling above us. I guess they'd decided to give us some privacy.

"Thirteen oh four," Opa said, repeating the address. We had no trouble finding it. It was a small stone home that the doctor had converted into an office. I pulled into the driveway and parked.

Finally. The end of the road. We simply sat there for awhile and listened to the ticking of the engine as it cooled.

Opa looked at me and tried to make it a light moment. "Thanks for the ride, Bud." Making it sound like I'd given him a lift across town.

"No problem."

"You drive better than most adults."

"Thanks."

"And you're a good traveling companion."

"So are you."

A curtain moved in one of the house's windows, and a woman peered out for a moment. Then she let the curtain fall. I'm sure she'd been following our progress on the news.

Opa said, "We'll go inside in a minute. Together. I think you should meet her. Unless you don't want to."

"I want to meet her."

Opa nodded. "I'm glad." Then he said, "Today's not the day, you know. Not yet. We still have some time together."

I'd been doing pretty well up until then. Keeping it under control. Not getting all emotional. But now I was beginning to lose it. Slowly. My bottom lip quivering. Tears forming. Then Opa leaning over to put an arm around my shoulders.

And that's where I'm going to end this part of the story, because even though our journey became the biggest media event of the summer, the conversation Opa and I had in those next few minutes is mine alone.

18

Hey Chuck

It was only a simple two-word text message, but it brought out my first real smile in several weeks. It was June 27 — a Tuesday — and I had been back in Abilene for four days.

Hey back. Good to hear from u. Then I added: *Been thinking about u.*

Really?

Every day.

Liar!

No its true. And it was.

U r sweet. How r u doing?

That was the question everyone had been asking me, and there was no short answer for it. Of course, everybody knew almost every detail about what had happened, because of the wall-to-wall coverage. It's hard to keep anything private nowadays. That was the drawback. The media had helped us complete our trip, but they had also attempted to elbow their way into everything that followed.

There had been no happy ending, of course. No magical last-minute treatment or miraculous recovery. Real life doesn't work that way.

Opa had chosen to die two weeks and five days after we'd arrived in Seattle.

I have no interest in describing his physical condition by that time, but I will say that any doubt I ever had about his choice had disappeared completely by that nineteenth day. I understand that there are people who could have been right there in the room with him in those final moments and still condemned his decision — and they are entitled to their opinion — but I will never agree with them.

That includes my parents. In fact, they *were* there. They saw what the disease had done to him. They offered as much love and emotional support as anyone can offer, but they never considered that maybe Opa had done the right thing. At least they were respectful enough to stop interfering after they'd flown up to Seattle. Opa had been worried that they'd try to get him declared incompetent so he couldn't follow through with his plan, but they hadn't done that. After all, they *are* honest people, and saying that Opa was mentally unstable would've been a lie.

Mom and I had flown home the day after Opa died, while Dad drove the Honda home. Opa's body stayed behind. He had chosen to be cremated, so that was being done in Seattle, and his ashes would be shipped to us later. He'd also left a letter addressed to me — not to Dad or Mom, but to me — with instructions on what he wanted done with his ashes.

Dear Bud,

Remember that conversation we had about being practical and rational? How there are times when you need to think logically and leave emotion out of it? That's true, of course, and both of us did that on our journey to Seattle. You know I'm grateful beyond words.

*But there are also times when practicality is a burden
and you must "think" with your heart. I bring this up
because I'm going to ask you for one more favor. In just
a few more years, you will be an adult, free to make all
of your own choices. I have no doubt that you will be the
type of caring, compassionate man that seems to be in
short supply in today's world.*

*When that day comes, I'd like for you to find a resting
place for my ashes. Where? That's up to you to decide.
Just jump in the Honda (it's yours now, by the way), take
a drive, and scatter the old man wherever you see fit.
Whatever feels right to you is fine with me. Will you do
that for me?*

With Love, Opa

I felt honored that he would ask. But I will admit that I was
a little intimidated by the request at first. This was a big
responsibility. Just spreading the ashes over some random lake
or up in the mountains didn't seem fitting. It took me awhile
to figure out what I needed to do, but as soon as the idea
occurred to me, I knew it was right. It wasn't just right, it was
perfect.

On my eighteenth birthday, I'd leave Abilene and drive
through Lubbock to Amarillo. See, just west of town, there's
a place with a bunch of old Cadillacs stuck nose first into the
ground. That seemed like an appropriate place to sprinkle
some of the ashes. After that, I'd continue west through
Albuquerque to Flagstaff. Then north to the Grand Canyon,
where'd I'd sprinkle a little more.

You get the idea.

I'd retrace the route we'd taken, remembering every
moment, good or bad, happy or heartbreaking. After all, that
trip was now as much a part of me as the color of my eyes and
the curls in my hair.

And, yes, regardless of how things went in the next few

years and the different directions life might take us, I thought it would be appropriate to stop in Salt Lake City and say hello to a new friend.

About The Author

Ben Rehder lives with his wife near Austin, Texas, where he was born and raised. *The Driving Lesson* is his eighth novel.

4210381R00096

Made in the USA
San Bernardino, CA
04 September 2013